Hashiye Par

Hashiye Par

FOR A TREE TO GROW

SHAILENDER SINGH

Translated from Dogri by
Suman K. Sharma

Edited by
Mini Krishnan

OXFORD
UNIVERSITY PRESS

OXFORD
UNIVERSITY PRESS

Oxford University Press is a department of the University of Oxford.
It furthers the University's objective of excellence in research, scholarship,
and education by publishing worldwide. Oxford is a registered trademark of
Oxford University Press in the UK and in certain other countries

Published in India
by Oxford University Press
YMCA Library Building, 1 Jai Singh Road, New Delhi 110 001, India

© Oxford University Press 2014

The moral rights of the authors have been asserted

First Edition published in 2014

ISBN-13: 978-0-19-945034-3
ISBN-10: 0-19-945034-X

Typeset in ITC Garamond Std 11/15.5
by Alphæta Solutions, Puducherry, India 605 009
Printed in India at Sapra Brothers, New Delhi 110 092

To
Indra

Contents

Author's Note

I am a policeman by profession and inquisitive by nature. My job requires me to reach out to the people in my precincts and keep myself aware of what is happening in the world around me.

A number of questions have plagued me since early youth. Is it not true that a third of our countrymen live below the 'poverty line'? And that even those who are a little more fortunate barely manage to hover between painful thrift and utter destitution? For such families to eke out a living is like enduring endless cycles of life and death several times before they actually pass away.

Noble Laureate, Amartya Sen has argued convincingly that it is possible even in deserts—where nature reveals its harshest face—to end starvation and poverty. Then, why, in a country like ours that is blessed with fertile lands and other resources, is there so much poverty? Is it because of an entrenched bias against certain classes of people? Or a faulty distribution of food supplies? These were the questions and reflections that troubled me and inspired me to take up the writing of a short story. While revisiting it, I found myself adding a few more things. These revisions expanded the work and it grew into a novel.

I have been to all the regions of the Jammu and Kashmir state, including the remote and most backward pockets, which like the rest of India, face the problem of grinding poverty despite its rich resources. My observations on the happenings around me took the shape of snippets and stories that I kept recording in a journal which I always carry with me. The present novel is borne out of those jottings.

I had started to write this novel in English but after ten-fifteen pages, it dawned on me that I was merely translating the words that came to my mind in Dogri. Felicity of a learnt language is not the same as the ease of expression in one's mother tongue. So I decided that the book should be written in Dogri and then translated into English. The decision facilitated a smooth flow of my feelings.

The original novel was published in 2010 under the title *Hashiye Par*. By a happy turn of events, I met Suman K. Sharma, a recognized author and translator from Jammu, who agreed to translate the book into English. I am grateful to Oxford University Press and in particular its Editor-Translations, Mini Krishnan, for affording it a wider reach.

The events described in *Hashiye Par* may well match the experiences in the life of any of my poverty-oppressed countrymen, but the novel is purely a work of imagination.

SHAILENDER SINGH

Translator's Note

As one among the growing number of aficionados of Dogri fiction, I too received an inscribed copy of *Hashiye Par* from Shailender Singh soon after the book was published in 2010. Little did I know then that a year later I would be asked to translate it into English.

I was pleased to get the offer and admittedly a little proud too. Pleased because of the opportunity it afforded me to make a fresh and compelling Dogri voice heard on the global stage, and proud that I had been singled out for the task. But my hubris soon gave way to humility as I went about the task. The book that to my reader's swift reading had appeared a simple enough narrative about a cause dear to the author's heart began to reveal its intricacies to my translatorial self. The first issue arose with the English title itself. A literal translation of *Hashiye Par* would have been *On the Margins*, which I thought would be too prosaic a title for such a remarkable work. I suggested *Beyond Reach* instead—drawing out the protagonist's futile efforts to receive the benefits extended by the state and the failure of the system itself to reach him. But the author did not agree with me.

There came a time when Shailender Singh came up with as many as twenty-two options to choose from. Not one of them appealed to me. We reached an impasse. The author said there was a 'gap of understanding' between us and I contended that if that was so, then it might be equally futile on my part to attempt a rendering of the work itself. It was at that juncture that Mini Krishnan stepped in with her immense editorial clout, telling both of us in plain English to reach an agreement rapidly or else the book would miss the publishing schedule. Then, taking a cue from the concluding paragraph of the novel, I made yet another suggestion—*For a Tree to Grow Tall.* The potted peepal plant can explode into its full potential only when it connects with the nourishing earth through one of its roots. It got Mini's ready approval, though not without excision of the redundant adjective 'tall'.

That was only the beginning. The narrative's rural tone repeatedly floored me. What was a *tuala*? Okay, for the literal meaning I could consult the Dogri-Hindi dictionary published by the Jammu and Kashmir Academy of Art, Culture and Languages. But I had never experienced the warmth of a roofless rustic hearth, which Madan, the protagonist, routinely shares with his wife Kanta and their children. Then there were other questions like when is paddy sown and harvested? How is a fishing line laid in the river? A toddler living in any village on the banks of the Chenab river could have easily described such things, but not me, a sixty-four-year-old Jammu-ite. Perhaps it would not be a very good excuse to say that I have been a city man all my life, for whom a village is a place of an occasional retreat from the city's noxious fumes and not somewhere one lives out the *real* business of life. Fortunately, the author Shailender Singh himself and friends like Chaman Panthi and Mohan Singh—eminent Dogri writers both—were always on hand to help me. Mohan Singh, scion of a traditional Rajput family, even took me to his ancestral village, Gurah Salathian a few miles from Jammu to give me the feel of a Dogra village. I still had to compromise on my reluctance to use footnotes to gloss some Dogri-specific expressions such as *tuala*, which refuse to budge from their native ethnicity.

Someone has said half-seriously that translation is a trucker's job—hauling baggage from one place to another. But not literary translations. They show the *attitude* of their authors—trifle with their identity or vivacity and you fail to carry them. I leave it to the worthy readers to judge how far I have succeeded in the task, but Mini Krishnan, my editor and my mentor, did not spare any effort in the endeavour. She encouraged me, she egged me on, and she honed my best efforts to improvise and improve my drafts. On more than one occasion she took it upon herself to successfully mediate between me and the author, and if she appeared to be taking sides with the translator, well that was what the affair was all about! It was her idea that the chapters should be given titles. To Mini, I record my everlasting gratitude. I am also grateful to Veena Gupta who recommended my name to Shailender Singh for the translation. To Lalit Magotra and Shashi Pathania go my thanks for the valuable insight into Dogri language, culture, and literature I gained from their scholarly writings. And finally who is more entitled to my thanks than Shailender Singh who despite the little and big differences that we had, never gave up on me.

SUMAN K. SHARMA

Introduction

For a Tree to Grow is a translation of Shailender Singh's Dogri novel *Hashiye Par* (literally, 'on the margins'). It is the tale of a *jheewar*[1] family living in an unnamed village on the banks of the Chenab river in the Indian state of Jammu and Kashmir. Thanks to the rigid caste system together with the geo-historical compulsions of the Dogras, not too long ago, the jheewars were treated as serfs and performed chores from cooking to dish-washing for the wealthy high-caste landowners. It was unthinkable for them to own farm land or get decent government jobs. The Dogra region, historically extending from the south of the Kashmir Valley to the north of the Pakistani province of Punjab and from the east of the Satluj river to the west of the Mannavar Tawi, has always been a hotbed of

1. A caste traditionally engaged in 'menial' tasks such as fishing, fetching water, and so on.

foreign invasions and internecine wars. Perforce, the warrior Rajputs became the dominant community in the region. The priestly class, those in trade and the peasants, however, retained their social importance because of the subsidiary functions they performed. Dalits such as the jheewars were relegated to performing menial tasks, and what might have started as a necessity became a terrible tradition. It took all the social engineering skills of the likes of Dr B.R. Ambedkar for Dalits in post-Independence India to empower themselves with education and to find their place in the sun.

Writing the original book in Dogri about a Dogra community seems to have been a judicious decision on the part of the author. The language imparts to the work gravity and authenticity of narration that perhaps would not have been possible in any other language. Of Indo-Aryan origin, Dogri has a recorded history of more than nine centuries. It was written in the Takri script, like Punjabi, and considered a dialect of that language till 1969 when it came to be recognized as an independent literary language. Now written in the Devanagari script like Hindi, it has been enshrined in the Indian constitution as one of the twenty-two major languages of the country. Noteworthy also is the initiative of the Central Institute of Indian Languages in preparing corpora of Dogri. The institute has produced and published *The Dogri Style Manual* in collaboration with the Dogri Sanstha, a voluntary organization dedicated to promote the language. The Department of Information Technology has, through C-DAC, uploaded on the internet software programmes and tools in Dogri containing over one hundred and fifty thousand statements and strings. IT-enabled, Dogri today can match any other language as a vehicle of expression.

A living language of antiquity, Dogri boasts of a rich literature. The verses of Manak Chand (*b.* 1565), Gambhir

Chand (*b*. 1690), and Kanshi Ram (1743–1836) might have gone out of popular memory, but the poems of Devi Ditta 'Dattu' (1723–1811)—who wrote in Brajbhasha with equal felicity—and Pandit Ganga Ram (1777–1858) still ring true. During the reign of Maharaja Ranbir Singh, books were written in the language on law, medicine, and army drill. A Dogri primer was prepared and Sanskrit works such as the Bhagavad Gita and *Leelavati*—an ancient treatise on mathematics—were translated. In 1944, Dogri Sanstha marked its advent with the publication of Dinu Bhai Pant's hilarious poem '*Shehr Pehlo Pehl Ge*' (The First Time We Went to the City). The first collection of Dogri short stories *Pehla Phull* (First Blossom) by Bhagwat Prasad Sathe came out three years later, though poetry remained for some time the Dogra literati's first love. The Dogri Sanstha published *Jaago Duggar* (Rise, Dogras!) in 1949 which is an anthology of poems by as many as seven poets—Har Datt, Dinu Bhai Pant, Ram Nath Shastri, Krishan Smailpuri, Parmanand Almast, Yash Sharma, and Ved Pal 'Deep'. The 1950s saw the emergence of new poets such as Kehri Singh Madhukar, Padma Sachdev, Tara Smailpuri, Shambhu Nath, Raghunath Singh Sambyal, and Ved Rahi. Short-story writers like Lalita Mehta, Ved Rahi, Narinder Khajuria, Madan Mohan Sharma, and Ram Kumar Abrol were also published during this period. Dogri prose too had had its heyday. Three novels published simultaneously in the 1960s by the authors Madan Mohan Sharma, Narinder Khajuria, and Ved Rahi, eight collections of essays, twenty-one translations of classical works, and a compilation of Dogri proverbs and idioms were some of the noteworthy works of that decade. Shivnath, a noted critic, observes in *Two Decades of Dogri Literature* (Sahitya Akademi, 1997) that while the output of Dogri books during the 1960s was below one hundred, it went up to three hundred during the eighth and ninth decades, averaging fifteen books a year—'a lean but steady streamlet—a phenomenon of troughs and tops, excellent pieces co-existing with puerile and absolutely mediocre stuff.' Two literary journals, *Nami Chetna* (New Awareness) brought out in 1953 by the Dogra Mandal, Delhi (later taken over by the Dogri Sanstha) and *Shiraza* started in 1964 by the Jammu and Kashmir Academy of Art, Culture and Languages contributed significantly to the promotion of Dogri literature.

Novel writing came late to Dogri literature. 'The development and growth of the Dogri novel has been rather slow and unsteady,' remarks Shivnath. In over fifty-three years of the first appearance of this genre in Dogri, there may not be as many novels published in the language. The novel entered the Dogri literary scene via the short story—Madan Mohan Sharma, Narinder Khajuria, and Ved Rahi were accomplished short-story writers before they experimented with novels. Second, Dogri novels are conspicuously rural in theme and content, perhaps because the Dogras primarily think agrarian. The first three Dogri novels—*Dhaaran te Dhooran* (Hills and Mists), *Shano* (titled after the protagonist's name), and *Haad, Bedi te Pattan* (The Flood, the Boat and the Landing)—are set in rural landscapes. Caught in the flux of a changing milieu, the characters rue their fate, but show no inclination to fight back. *Bukkh* (Hunger) by Shivdev Susheel and *Jeevan Daan* (Gift of Life) by Tara Daanpuri are about social discrimination in rural society and its aftermath, but puerile idealism mars their overall effect. *Phull Bin Daali* (Bloom Without a Branch) by Vats Vikal published in 1970, took up the cause of widow remarriage in a rural setting. Deshbandhu Dogra's three novels—*Qaidi* (The Prisoner, 1980), *Piyoke Bhejo* (Send Me to My Parents' Home, 1984), and *Jaangali Lok* (Wild Folks,

1987)—deal with various facets of village life. Even Shivdev Singh Sushil's novels *Bakkhre Bakkhre Sach* (Everyone has His Own Truth) and *Khali Ambar* (Void Skies) assay depiction of modern life in rustic environments. The exceptions are O.P. Sharma Saarthi's oeuvre and Narsingh Dev Jamwal's *Bin Kandhaan da Kotha* (A House without Walls). Saarthi's novels—*Treh Samundar Di* (Thirst of an Ocean), *Nanga Rukh* (translated into English by Shivnath under the title '*Churning of the City*'), *Makaan* (The House), *Patthar te Rang* (Stone and Colour), *Resham de Keedey* (Silkworms), and *Apna Apna Suraj* (For Everyone His Own Sun)—all are symbolic as is Jamwal's novel. But then both Saarthi and Jamwal concentrate on the psychological and inward journeys of their characters rather than the external world.

Hashiye Par is a welcome addition to Dogri fiction, as we shall see presently. Madan, the protagonist, is a Dalit who lives with his family on the fringe of an unnamed village. Dismally poor, he has dreams of a better life—a well-lit cement house that is secure against the vagaries of weather, a good education for his children ensuring jobs in the government when they grow up, and adequate food for all of them throughout the year and so on. Then the narrative departs from tradition. The sufferings and exploitation that he and his father had to endure at the hands of the upper-caste landowners are but bitter memories of the past. There is no longer a *direct* confrontation or bad blood between him as a jheerwar and his upper caste compatriots. On the other hand, when his eldest son Kamal shows promise in his studies, everyone in the adjoining town applauds the boy's success. Kamal's class teacher even buys him books and counsels him to work still harder. Thanks to his own diligence and the determination of the whole family, Kamal not only secures admission in an engineering college but is also awarded a scholarship to continue his studies.

Madan, who was despised only a few years ago even by the school children for the foul smell of fish that clung to him like a shameful badge of his lowly status, becomes Madan, the respected father of Kamal, the village boy who has brought honour to the whole town. Kamal's well-rewarded success in academics serves as a foil to Madan's dismal failure to get his due—the government 'money cheque' for building a pukka house. What the author seems to imply is that there is nothing particularly wrong with the system as it exists today—the fault lies with its implementation. The dispossessed can obtain what is rightfully theirs by getting 'connected with the earth … to regularly draw sustenance' (p. 133) like a growing tree.

Shailender Singh is realistic enough to suggest that the world order does not offer any free lunches. Everyone has to make a conscious choice and then to exert himself so to achieve the desired end. Madan's resolve to foreswear *bidi*-smoking comes from his 'zestful wish to live a healthy and fulfilling life' (p. 9). When Kanta raises the idea of share-cropping, it is with the intention of providing enough food for their children who 'eat like adults' (p. 96). Kamal studies hard because he wants 'his starving family to have, instead of a worn-out hut, a pukka brick and mortar house …' (p. 128). To borrow from Amartya Sen's terminology, each member of the family uses his or her 'capabilities' to shift from 'economic unfreedom' to a freedom to live the life they want to live. The achievement of *Hashiye Par* lies in perceiving a trend of global significance in the humdrum existence of a marginalized family of the Jammu region.

SUMAN K. SHARMA

Winter and Sunshine

It was six in the morning on a freezing day in January. Darkness filled the air as if it was midnight.

Cascading down the mountains, the Chenab flowed gently into the plains. The river spewed silt on both banks, imparting a new colour to the soil and a new vitality to the fields for the crops to grow. About a kilometre and a half from the river towards the north, lay a sleepy village of a hundred dwellings, cradling in its lap about six hundred souls. The biting cold drove the cattle to huddle together under the sheds. Street dogs slept in their haunts tucking their nose-tips under their tails.

In one corner of the village stood a hut made of cane and *saroot* grass. Its six-seven metre thatch was clearly visible under the moonlight. The hut had no walls; instead canes and blades cut to size stood planted in the ground. In the centre of both sides were split bamboos tied with jute ropes. That was all Madan had for a house.

As he woke up, Madan pulled down the quilt from his face and found that his eldest son, Kamba, had bundled himself up and was clinging to him. It was Madan's body heat that had kept the boy warm, otherwise he would not have clung to him.

On another cot, swathed in a tattered quilt, lay Madan's two daughters, Kamlesh and Usha. That the thin quilt saved them from the cold was doubtful, but they lay huddled in the centre of the cot. On a separate cot close to Madan's was his wife, Kanta, with their infant son, Louku.

Madan flipped back the quilt, emerged from under it and sat on the cot which creaked *chdooon*, as if to say that it, too, was awake now. He lowered his feet to the ground and felt for his rubber shoes in the darkness. He first dug his toes into the pair and then his heels. The shoes were stone-hard because of the extreme cold. Madan stood up. An icy draught of air chilled him to the bone; goosebumps appeared all over him. Madan turned back and carefully wrapped the quilt around Kamba. Bending down to pick up a *loi*[1] from the bed, he stood up again. Unfolding one end of the loi and unfurling it, he wrapped himself up to brave the chill outside.

The saroot hut was surrounded by cane fencing keeping out birds and bigger animals, but allowed mice, lizards, and other pests to pass through at will. The chilly wind of the winter blew lazily, icing up everything that lay inside.

Kanta too had woken up, as was her daily routine. Instinctively, she extended her hand to reach out to her left side

---

1. A light blanket.

and covered baby Louku under the quilt. The child had been exposed in his sleep. Her own face covered fully under the quilt, she listened to the faint sounds Madan was making. There was no need for her to leave the bed yet. She uncovered her face a little and following the direction of the sounds made by her husband, peered at his receding back in the darkness. Rays of moonlight coming through chinks pierced the darkness in the hut.

In two or three strides, Madan approached the gash in the front wall, which served both as the exit and entry to his hut. Bending forward, he lifted the cover from it and put it aside. He stepped out, lifted the cover again and secured it against the opening as if the flimsy contrivance could banish the chill that vexed his family.

He took a step backwards and stood up. The thump of Madan's hardened shoes echoed in the morning stillness as he walked towards the river. Kanta listened attentively to her husband's receding footfalls till she lost the sound to the increasing distance.

Madan warmed up as he walked, increasing his pace. The moonlight made the fog visible and the icy wind seemed to pierce the body where it came in contact with any exposed part.

On that cold desolate morning, it did not take Madan long to reach the Chenab. On the river's surface flowed another river of fog, formed by tiny droplets of ice-cold water. The white fog shone like silver in the moonlight. Madan tightened the folds of his blanket and flung it on his shoulders, forming a shallow bag in front of him. Then he bent down and folded both the legs of his pajamas right up to his knees. Taking off his shoes at the edge of the water, he stepped into the river with great fortitude.

The Chenab takes its shape from the molten ice of the mountains of the Doda and Kishtwar ranges along with the waters of the Chandra Bhaga tributaries. When it reaches this spot, its temperature barely touches two-three degrees Celsius. Madan's legs grew numb in a matter of moments as he pulled at the first plastic handline. It had a single fish on it. Holding the fish in his right hand, he sought out the hook. He gave the hook a twist with his left hand and pulled it out of the fish's mouth. The fish writhed in his hand. Madan put it in the makeshift bag he had held against his chest. The fish grew still as soon as it was put into the bag.

Madan picked up the second line and popped those fishes into his bag. In this manner, one by one, he pulled out all the lines. Some hooks had caught fish, some not, as the smarter of the fish had eaten the bait and gone free. Recovering all the fishing tackle, Madan came out of the water. The rather long spell in the water had left wrinkles on his feet. He shook the water off from both his feet and put on his rubber shoes.

Madan's limbs remained numb for some time, even after he had left the river. The air outside warmed him and gave him a pleasant sensation. He shook the fishes he had caught and made them into a parcel to carry home.

The day was breaking, making the path to home more visible. The soft light also showed Madan's face: his three-day old stubble, sunken cheeks, a large fleshy nose under luster-less eyes, and a dark complexion.

Walking home, as the soles of his shoes rubbed off the dew on the grass, he carried himself like a hunting dog bounding towards its catch. It did not take him long to cover the distance of one and a half kilometres.

Madan had erected a *tuala*[2]—a mud construction of about two and half feet high—on the right side of the door. The enclosure was painted not with lime but *parola*, a fine-grained earth of a shade of grey. Inside the tuala was the family *chulha*, a wood-burning earthen stove. The chulha too had been painted on the outside with parola.

Standing against the tuala's wall was a rack for storing clay pitchers. It always had one pitcher that had to be intact and held two more pitchers which were old, their necks partially broken. The sand below the rack was often wet with the water that spilled while being drawn from the pitchers. Adjacent to the pitcher rack, behind the tuala, was a basin for washing dishes.

Outside the hut, on the left side was the family compound. Kanta had plastered it with a layer of fine ground earth and a thin coating of cow dung paste. On the sides, she had skilfully drawn borders with parola.

Kanta saw Madan as he reached the lane adjoining their hut. It was broad daylight now.

Madan walked over from the lane to his compound and taking a few steps more, approached the tuala. He placed the parcel of fish on the low tuala wall and went to the hearth, where Kanta was trying to light up a fire with little pieces of firewood and last evening's embers that she had left buried in the ash. The small fire did not give off much warmth in the beginning. Usually, Madan would pass his hands momentarily over the fire and pull them back, but as the bigger pieces of wood in the chulha caught fire it began to emit more heat.

---

2. A roofless enclosed space adjacent to the living room used for cooking and eating.

The growing warmth spread pleasurably through Madan. He felt his limbs loosening up.

Kanta fed the fire with tinder the moment she found it weakening; it now burned strongly. The chulha had become hot enough. Kanta picked up an aluminium pot and placed it on the chulha.

* * *

After Madan had left his bed early in the morning, the quilt had steadily lost its warmth and Kamba's body was shrinking into itself to conserve heat. The boy was cold. Having lost his sleep because of the chill, he saw that his father had returned from his morning errand and that there was a fire in the chulha. Rubbing his eyes, he got out of bed and approached the chulha barefoot.

'You should have remained in bed, son. Why have you come out in this chill?' Kanta asked when she saw Kamba huddling close to her.

But Kamba pushed himself between Kanta and Madan in an effort to earn himself a place closest to the fire. Madan moved aside a little and said, 'Come, sit here.'

Kanta took out little packets of tea leaves and sugar from a plastic bag. Lifting the lid, she put some tea leaves and sugar into the pot and replaced the lid.

'How good was the catch today?' she asked, glancing at the parcel.

'There are two big ones, a few medium-sized, and some small ones too.'

Madan pushed the log into the fire. Kanta rose to her feet, went inside and returned in a short while with half a glass of milk and two empty glasses. She uncovered the pot again and added milk to the tea. She quickened the fire. The tea came to another boil and was ready.

Lifting the pot with the corner of her head cloth, she began to pour the tea into three glasses.

'Is there any *roti* around here?' Madan asked for the rotis that might have been left uneaten the previous night.

'Yes, we have two,' replied Kanta.

After pouring tea into the glasses, Kanta got up again and went into the hut. Inside, their other children lay asleep. She brought back two rotis wrapped in a filthy kitchen napkin. The three picked up their glasses. Madan got one roti, while Kanta and Kamba shared the other.

Finishing their tea, they continued to sit close to the chulha to let the gentle warmth seep into their bodies for a little longer.

The sun had risen and the fog was receding gradually. The sunrays touched the ground and warmed the grass. As the dew on the grass evaporated, its vapours rose in a delicate patina.

Madan got up, stretched and took a deep breath. Then he picked up the packet of fish from the alcove in wall and set out for his second errand of the day.

Passing through the bylanes of his village, he walked alone as usual on the rough stretch of the untarred road, to sell his fish in the town, which was two kilometres away. The village children, dressed in their tidy uniforms, also went along the same path to their school. But they kept their distance from him. Some walked ahead and others followed him. That was nothing new for Madan. He had a fair idea of his clothes and appearance. The school children shunned him because his clothes reeked of fish. He didn't mind the stink himself as he had grown accustomed to it.

Though they despised him, Madan was fond of looking at the children going to their school. He hoped that one day his own children would also go to school, or even to the city college for higher studies. He was ready to do anything to give his children a good education.

Last year, Madan recalled, how one day, on his way to sell fish in the city, as usual, he was accompanied by his cousin, Tarsem. They were talking to each other when Madan took out a bundle of *bidi*s from his pocket and picking out one, put it between his lips and lit it up. Tarsem asked him, 'How many bidis do you smoke in a day?'

'Just one bundle,' Madan had replied. Tarsem had popped another question, 'How much does a bundle cost?'

Was that a question to ask! Madan had pondered for a while. Everybody knew the cost of a Ganesh Bidi bundle. 'It costs three rupees,' he had replied and taken a deep puff after supplying the information.

Tarsem had looked at Madan with concern and said, 'It means you spend three rupees every day on bidis. That would be ninety rupees in a month and more than a thousand a year.'

Madan was stunned to learn that every year he had been spending more than a thousand rupees on just bidis. He had never calculated his expenses beyond one or two days. On Tarsem's revelation, he felt as if he had been caught committing a serious blunder.

Tarsem, on his part, looked satisfied because he had wanted Madan to see the folly of his ways. Tarsem had driven home his point. 'If you really want,' he had told Madan, 'you can save this thousand rupees a year and spend the money on your children's education. And in the bargain, you will stop ruining your health as well.'

The sorry expression on Madan's face at realizing his fault was suddenly replaced by a zestful wish to live a healthy and fulfilling life. Tarsem had put him on the right track.

It came to Madan's mind that being educated did have its merits. He had never bothered about what he had been spending on his bidis. From that day on, Madan had stopped buying bidis at his own expense, though he couldn't refuse if someone else offered him one once in a while. It was a matter of time before he had overcome the habit altogether.

Madan had realized that although there were many other educated people in the village, no one else had shown him such deep sympathy and advised him in such a telling manner.

Madan's trust in Tarsem was complete. Tarsem's father, Shailo Ram, had also been poor. But he had not allowed the lack of means to come in his way in providing for Tarsem's education.

Tarsem had become a teacher in a secondary school two years ago. Madan also nursed a secret desire that, like Tarsem, his own children should get the best education available, and on growing up, secure themselves good government jobs. That was the reason Madan had quit bidi-smoking.

Looking at the children on their way to school, and indulging in flights of fancy as usual, he reached the city. Thoru's *dhaba*[3] was located half the way through the bazaar. The town had two eateries, and the other one was also close by. All the buses passing through the town had a stopover at these dhabas, and Thoru's place was the more popular of the two because not only the city passengers but also the bus crews preferred to eat there.

As Thoru swept the garbage out of his dhaba, Madan sat waiting on a sun-drenched bench outside. Thoru made a heap of bits of bone, spilled-over rice and dal in the middle of the bazaar road. He went back into his shop to replace

3. Roadside eatery.

the broom. Folding an old newspaper three or four times, he made a fan of sorts and sat opposite an oven. Bits of waste paper and splinters of packing wood were already there at the bottom of the oven. On this tinder Thoru packed coal and fired the oven. White smoke billowed from the oven and filled the shop, depositing soot on its already blackened walls and ceiling. With the make-do, hand-held fan, Thoru maintained an energetic supply of air through the vent of the oven. The air forced through the oven enhanced the flames and generated noxious fumes.

Both Thoru and his servant Panju were firing an oven each. Frequently, when the smoke blew into their faces, they would stop fanning to cough and splutter before they resumed their fanning all over again.

Thoru was a paunchy, dark-skinned man of average height. He had a bulbous nose, thick dark lips, and curly hair and smelled of the liquor that he had drunk the previous night. The smoke had turned his red eyes even redder.

After a while the ovens stopped smoking and began to blaze. There was no more smoke now. Thoru got up and sat on the long bench inside the shop.

Madan approached Thoru and sitting beside him on the same bench, opened his parcel of fish. Thoru picked up the biggest fish and after examining it thoroughly, weighed it and threw it into an empty vessel placed before him. In the same manner, he threw the other fish into the vessel. His hands had become sticky with the fluids of the dead fish. He wiped his hands on his kurta and taking out a wad of currency notes from his pocket, pulled out two fifty-rupee notes and gave them to Madan.

'Panju, clean the fish,' Thoru instructed his servant.

Madan spent another ten minutes talking to Thoru before leaving his shop. Walking through the bazaar, he arrived at Desu's grocery shop. People called the shopkeeper 'Desu Shah'.[4] Madan climbed the two low steps and went into the shop. Desu Shah was seated on a *takhtposh*—a wide, low wooden platform—on the left side of the shop. On his left was placed his money chest and on his right were piled five or six long, red-bound books which contained records of the loans he had advanced.

Desu Shah, a trim man in his mid-sixties, presented a sleek look in his spotless white kurta and pajama. His oil-smeared silvery hair glistened over the oblong vermillion mark on his forehead and toothless sunken cheeks. He sat cross-legged below the pictures of the Goddess Lakshmi and Lord Ganesha, which were garlanded with fresh marigold flowers. Incense sticks burning under the pictures of the deities filled the shop with a mild fragrance.

With bowed head, Madan said namaste to Desu Shah before he sat down on a bench on the right.

Desu Shah was talking to some customers. He nodded cursorily to Madan and asked the other men to continue.

'Is it true that *Mantriji* is coming tomorrow to address a huge gathering?' asked one customer.

'Yes, the minister is coming,' replied Desu Shah.

'And, they say, he will personally hand out money cheques to all the poor, homeless families so that they build them-selves brick houses,' he added.

'Will the Minister be distributing money cheques with his own hands?' another amazed customer asked.

4. The term 'shah' could mean either a trader or a money-lender.

Denigrating the villager's awed expression Desu Shah said, 'You see, there are hardly a few months left for the election. The ministers and others in power are doing all these things to attract voters.'

Other customers who sat there readily supported Desu Shah's statement.

'They have done nothing in this period of four long years. Now that the election is coming, they are in a hurry to do everything at once,' said Desu Shah, reinforcing his statement.

Desu Shah, like the customers talking to him, was opposed to the ruling party.

Madan listened to the men quietly. All his concentration was focused on just one point—news of government assistance for the homeless poor, money for a brick house. Madan expected that they would say more about it. But to his dismay, Desu Shah had cut short the conversation with his acerbic comment.

Madan's mind raced with ideas. 'How nice of mantriji! He wants to build pukka houses for us poor and homeless! Does it really matter that elections are at hand? What does that Shah know of the pain and shame of living in a hut of mud and reeds! Winter comes like a frosty demon and its nightly chill squeezes us to the bone. Rains make life miserable. Icy draughts pierce our tattered blankets and ragged quilts like a thousand knives. In summer, strong winds at dusk threaten to blow the hut away. Dust in the bed, dust in food, and dust in the eyes. Dust and nothing but dust everywhere. There can be no light in the clay lamp and no fire in the hearth; tinder as it is, one gust of wind is enough to set the hut ablaze. I often have to sleep on an empty stomach, and so does my wife. But it rends my heart to see the little ones going to bed hungry. My wife can cook only when the winds subside.

But awful it is to wake children at midnight and ask them to eat.' Madan was sunk in thought when Sohan asked him, 'What will you buy?'

Sohan was Desu Shah's son and everybody called him 'Sunna'. Desu Shah spent his days on the *takht*, talking to the customers and keeping accounts of money he had lent and received. It was Sunna who actually ran the grocery store.

Madan asked Sunna for flour, sugar, and oil supplies to last for a day and a half. Sunna weighed out the rations on the scales. By that time the other customers had left and Desu Shah was busy reading an Urdu newspaper. Madan handed over the currency notes to him, received the balance and after exchanging courtesies once again, came out of the shop.

Carrying the bag of rations in his left hand and swathing himself with the loi with his right, Madan stepped down the raised platform of the shop and proceeded towards his home.

The sun was climbing the skies. The morning chill was waning because of the sunshine. Once again, Madan fell to thinking of the government's plan for pukka houses[5] for the homeless poor and the minister's impending visit to distribute cheques. If the government was providing money to the poor for building brick houses, couldn't he, Madan, be a beneficiary? By the next winter, he might well be living in his own brick house, like his neighbour Birumal did. His family would then enjoy the comfort and prestige of sleeping behind doors and windows barred against the chill. They would have a crackling fire inside the room to make rotis as well as to keep themselves warm. No more would the icy winds harass them. He also thought of the MLA of the area and of the people

_____

5. Unlike a hut, a 'pukka house' is a brick-and-cement house.

in the government. They had to be good. It was because of
them that this was going to happen.

Deep in these thoughts, Madan did not know that he had
already crossed the bazaar.

Madan's fancies rapidly built a pukka house before his
eyes. He anticipated the comforts of living in a proper house.
In the summer, the family would keep the windows open to
beat the heat. When the days turned windy, they would close
every door and every window. No longer would the children
have to sleep on empty stomachs just because it was too
windy to light a fire. The monsoons would not leave the roof
leaking. If, perchance, the entire family had to go anywhere,
they could lock their door and leave.

Madan's musings took him back to his childhood.

A House of Dreams

As a child Madan had lived with his family in a small saroot hut built in a corner of the village. As early as summer, his mother plastered the chinks in the cane fence—which was not an easy job, but she was deft at it. She would take a blob of wet clay and placing it gently against the cane fence, press its corners to the canes till it stuck fast. Madan and his younger siblings tried to copy her, but they could never succeed. Madan's father, Sardari Lal, would bring basketfuls of clay from afar. He would heap the clay on the ground and the whole family would sit pounding it to a fine consistency. A little crater would then be made in the centre of the heap and water poured into it. The playful part in this activity was kneading the sticky mud with their feet, in which Madan and his siblings participated happily. Frequently, Sardari Lal would shoo them away. 'Get lost,' he would say in mock anger, 'don't you have anything else to do?'

The children would go away for a while, only to return to squelching mud all over again.

Madan would use bits of the wet clay to fashion wheels and bodies of toy motorcars and dry them in the sun. By sunset, the little shapes would have dried and he would seek his father's help to assemble the parts into moveable little vehicles. Sardari Lal would be only too willing to oblige his son, because he had never been able to buy his children any toys. He buried the mud toys in the ashes of the family chulha where the heat would bake the toys brick-hard. Children then tied strings to their clay-motors and dragged them wherever they went.

Some five or six kilometres from the village lived Madan's naani, who was very fond of him. He too liked to visit her with his mother. On such occasions Mother used to sit close to her own mother and naani, whose eyesight was weak, would ask him to draw near so she could see how well he was growing.

Naani could not have been sixty, but with her skeletal build and face furrowed like a dry date, she looked a hundred years old. She generally wore a dirty white cloth loosely tied about herself. Madan's maami, who was busy all day long with household chores, would leave everything else to be with them. She would bow to touch Mother's feet and Mother would ask her to rise and hug her. The women would then sit talking together, while Madan went out to play with his three cousins.

Madan's uncle would come home at dusk and everybody would eat before sunset. When it grew dark, they all slept in a saroot hut. They did not miss being in a pukka house as no one in Madan's widest circle of kinship owned one. All the other workmen and their families in that region lived exactly like they did.

Growing up, Madan saw his parents gradually growing feeble and steadily losing their capacity to work. He also saw some of the villagers growing prosperous. Their huts were replaced by one- or two-room pukka houses; Madan's family only grew larger. His siblings got married and started their own families in separate huts, though his parents continued to live in their old hut.

A year ago, Mother began to run a fever. When Madan went to enquire about her health, his father, Sardari Lal, said wistfully, 'If only we had a pukka house, we might have spent our last days in a little comfort.'

'No one in our entire clan has got a pukka house, then how can *we* hope to have one!' Mother had said with a deep sigh.

Madan thought about his relatives. Mother was right. It was a different matter that their relatives lived in bigger huts and some of them had two huts instead of just one. The only exception was Tarsem, who had bought bricks for his house, but even he had not been able to build a pukka house so far.

* * *

So wrapped in his memories was Madan, that he did not quite know when he had completed the journey home from the city.

Handing over the paper bag to Kanta, he said, 'Give me something to eat. I am famished.'

'I have given the last night's leftovers of rice and fish curry to the children for their breakfast. I too am hungry. It was you I was waiting for,' Kanta replied.

There was flour in the paper bag. Kanta bent low to enter the opening into the hut. She measured out flour from the paper bag and began to sift it in the sieve, while Madan tried to revive the chulha fire with little pieces of firewood.

Having kneaded the dough, Kanta rolled it into a ball to one side of the basin and washed her hands. By that time Madan had set off a crackling fire in the chulha. Seeing that his wife had washed her hands, he placed a *tava*[1] on the chulha. Kanta brought the dough to the tuala, but appeared to have forgotten something. She went into the hut again with the swiftness of an eagle and brought back the rolling board, roller, and some dry flour on a platter to firm up the soggy dough.

Kanta rolled out a roti and flattening it with her palms, threw it flat on the hot pan. She hardened the perfectly round roti by flipping it from one side to the other. Taking it off the pan, she baked the roti on an open flame and put it in a grubby basket by her side.

Having baked two rotis, Kanta ladled out two pieces of fish and some thin gravy from an aluminium pot into a dish and gave it to Madan. Madan accepted the dish from her and took the rotis from the basket. He tore off a piece and dipping it in the fish curry, popped it eagerly into his mouth and began to chew it.

While eating, Madan's mind was engrossed with several things at once, though hunger had made him too feeble to speak. But a couple of rotis revived him and still munching, he told Kanta that the following day was a Sunday and that the Mantriji himself was visiting the town to address a large gathering there.

'Why is he coming?' Kanta raised her head to ask.

---

1. Flat iron pan used for baking roti/chapatti.

'He is coming here to distribute cheques to all the poor and homeless so that they can have their own pukka houses,' Madan replied, looking at Kanta.

Kanta was excited about the distribution of money for building pukka houses. Her face beamed with happiness. Her family was poor. They didn't have a pukka house—only a saroot-and-cane hut to live in. Now they too would receive a cheque for building a pukka house. Had not they already registered their names with the Block Committee when a count was taken of the homeless in the village! Turning a roti on the pan, Kanta said to Madan, 'We'll hire masons to build our house.'

Munching on his roti, Madan affirmed, 'Yes, we will.'

Kanta had begun to fantasize. 'We won't hire any labourer,' she continued.

'Of course, not.' Madan nodded in agreement.

Kanta went on, 'I will get up early in the morning to do the cooking, rush through other chores and be ready to assist you in the construction of the house.'

The happiness of the days to come could be read on her radiant face. Her long nose seemed unusually prominent on her thin face as she gushed, 'I have wished for so long to have our home lit by an electric lamp so that our Kamba, Kamlesh, and Usha too could study till late in the night like Gulchain Singh's children.'

Madan listened to his wife so attentively that his munching slowed. In his wife's spoken desires he heard the echo of his own.

Having had his fill, Madan stopped eating. He came out of the tuala and went to the pitcher rack to draw a glass of water. He took one or two sips and gargled noisily before spitting into the open. Gargling a few more times, he rinsed his hands and came back, holding the glass.

He looked at his hut and noticed that it had begun to rot at the top. After two monsoons interspersed by stark sunshine, the once golden *kharh* straws of the thatch had rotted and turned black. To provide a new roof during the coming rains, Madan thought, he would have to go to the nearest ravine in a couple of weeks and cut sufficient quantities of ripe saroot grass. He calculated that if a pukka room could be built before the rains, he would not have to bother thatching the hut again.

Kanta baked two rotis for herself and with a burning log pushed the tava off the fire, standing it against the wall. Sitting down to eat, she began to think again about her dream house.

'Our house will stand on the vacant land beyond the tuala. It will have a window opening to the lane,' she said while chewing her food.

'That would be nice. The electric pole is close by in the lane,' Madan agreed with her readily.

Madan said he would dig the foundations himself and do all the manual work of which he was capable. He thought of all the possibilities of saving money in the construction of the house. Getting cheap timber for roof beams would be easy, he hoped.

People in the area generally used the timber that floated down the river when it was in the spate. Young swimmers caught big logs and hid them from government officials. They buried the timber to sell it at an opportune time. The stolen logs went at less than half their market price.

'Just one round to the adjoining village by both of us would be enough to provide mud to erect brick walls,' said Kanta, voicing her thoughts. Madan responded with a nod. The couple went on planning the construction of their brick house.

It was dusk. Madan grew impatient waiting for the next day to dawn. Blood pounding in his veins, he felt a new surge of enthusiasm. He wished the day would pass quickly because on Sunday, that fell the following day, he would receive a cheque for the construction of his house.

It was to be a big day in the lives of Kanta and Madan. With the sole exception of Tarsem who had stored bricks for building himself a room or two, none of their relatives owned a house with a pukka room. They were all people who could not even imagine what it felt like to own a pukka house.

Madan was born in a saroot hut. He had grown up and got married in the very saroot hut which had sheltered his entire family. When it was time for him to find a home for his own family, it was a hut again that he had built with the help of his older brother.

Not that he had any option. Madan subsisted on the paltry sums he got from selling fish, or an occasional day's wage as a labourer. His family owned no farming land. Their plot was less than 150 square yards in a corner of the village, which was barely sufficient for a growing family to live on. Beyond that they received small gifts when there was a wedding in the family of a landlord of the village, or when Kanta earned a few rupees washing dishes at the weddings. With no regular income, Kanta and Madan could never have saved the money to build a house.

Where would they get an income? They had no inheritance, no land to farm, no art or craft of an artisan, and no education that would earn them a government job. Madan had to earn something by manual labour every single day to keep the fire burning in his hearth.

Madan relived a fifteen to twenty-year old scene from his boyhood days when his father, Sardari Lal, had not yet lost his vitality and was capable of very hard work. It was his job to fetch drinking water from the river for everyone who worked in the fields under the scorching July-August sun in the harvesting season. Sardari Lal could be recognized at a great distance—a pitifully thin man in a dirty white kurta, a dhoti of the same colour, a red cotton scarf thrown over his shoulders, and his *behngi*.[2] Between the river and the fields where the farmhands toiled, his swaying yoke kept time with every step that he took, dancing as it were to some strange music. The swaying behngi was Sardari Lal's identity. He did not hold a sickle but quenched the thirst of all the farmhands of Zaildar Dayaram with the soothingly cold waters of the river Chenab.

2. A yoke with pitchers fastened at both ends.

A Labour of No Love

Zaildar Dayaram, the biggest landowner in the region, lived in a mansion proportionate to his status. It was his custom to go to his farms at the times of sowing and reaping. He also visited his farms at least once a week to view the lush crops.

It was high noon. Zaildar Dayaram was ready to go to his farms. His fifty-odd years sat lightly on him. Assertive in his white turban, immaculate kurta-pajama and black leather *juttis*, he commanded his servant, 'Saddle the horse and bring it here.'

He approached the mare and mounted her in a single leap. The servant handed over the reins. Zaildar Dayaram pulled the reins and goaded the mare with his heels. In an instant the animal began to gallop spiritedly.

As a boy, Madan had taken to going to the fields to give his father a helping hand. It was the month of Baisakh

(April-May) and having completed one round of carrying water from the river when it was a scorching forty to forty-two degrees, Sardari Lal was resting a while under the shade of a tree. Madan could be seen bringing water from the river all by himself. The behngi swayed from his shoulders as he proceeded on his path. Watching his son from a distance, Sardari Lal felt proud—the boy too had become adept at serving others. Presently, Madan approached him. Sardari Lal walked with him towards the fields where the farmhands were busy reaping the crops.

From there, they saw a man astride a black mare riding towards them at full gallop from the direction of the village. Everybody knew it was Zaildar Dayaram. The mare halted near the workmen.

'Sardari Lal, who is this boy? I haven't seen him before.' Zaildar Dayaram asked, looking at Madan closely.

'*Mai baap*,[1] he is my son,' replied Sardari Lal, joining both his hands together as a mark of respect.

'Bravo, Sardari Lal! You have trained your son in good time,' saying this, Zaildar Dayaram dug his heels into his mount once again and was gone.

Sardari Lal was elated and his narrow chest expanded. It was rare for a workman to get such recognition from the zaildar, and that too when the big landowner was mighty pleased. Sardari Lal had another reason to be happy. Only a few days earlier, Zaildar Dayaram had got angry with his cousin, Shailo Ram. Tarsem, Shailo Ram's son, had passed the eighth grade and in a moment of joy Shailo Ram had taken the boy to the

---

1. A term from the feudal times, roughly translated as 'you are my Mother and Father', implying total subservience and loyalty.

zaildar to seek his blessings. Father and son had stood before the zaildar deferentially.

'Shailo Rama, what's the matter? Why have you come here?' The Zaildar had enquired briskly.

'Mai baap, my son has passed the eighth grade. You know with what difficulty I have seen him through his studies. Could you put in a kind word to Mansukh Ray Sahib, the MLC, to get him a job? You are everything to us, mai baap,' Shailo Ram had spluttered all in one breath.

'Shailo Rama, what are you blabbering about?' shouted Zaildar Dayaram, 'It's all right for your children to read and write. But if your sons go on to take government jobs, who will do the work that you jheewars do? If things go on like this, it is a matter of days before our village goes without a workman. Now get out of my sight. And take your son with you. Tell him to assist you in what you do here.'

Shailo Ram had felt dejected. He knew that Zaildar Dayaram was right. It was not in the fate of his kin to find a government job; such jobs were meant for the big people. God had willed it like that. Or else why would he have been a jheewar and not a Brahmin? To serve others was his dharma, his prime duty. There was great merit in it. God was with those who did their duty. Reasoning with himself thus, he had gone back to his home with his son.

Tarsem had followed his father wordlessly, but his mind was in turmoil. He, an educated boy, would never consent to pick up and clean the dishes fouled by drunkards. Why should he have to go to other peoples' homes to do odd jobs, fetch them water, and render them services which demeaned him? If such things indeed brought a person merit and God's favour, then why didn't people like the zaildar themselves earn

such merit? Why didn't they do their own work and assist
others to please God? It was all a lie, thought Tarsem, a sham
to fool poor working people. But he dared not utter a word
before Zaildar Dayaram.

For a few days, both Sardari Lal and Madan floated on the
thin air of the zaildar's words of praise for their menial work.
They would race in the high noon to fetch water from the
river and serve it to the farmhands all across the vast farm-
lands. The temperature was pushing forty-five degree Celsius
and the workers sweating it out in the burning sun felt rejuve-
nated with a refreshing drink of water. It was hard work picking up every single wheat straw and severing it from its stock,
then frog-marching to the next wheat stock and so on. That
frog-march under the blazing sun in the vast open field! Their
skin not only darkened; it also blistered and burned under
the unsparing sun. The day-long perspiration left a worker
broken in both mind and body by evening. And on the top of
it, he returned home empty handed without the day's wages!
Those men still thought it was a privilege working for Zaildar
Dayaram. Just because he was a big man.

During the wedding feasts of the big farmers, Sardari Lal
made it a point to reach the place early in the morning. Madan
also started accompanying him after he had left his boyhood
behind. Their first task in the morning was to draw water
from the well and scrub cauldrons, frying pans and pots in
preparation for the community feast. Then a *dahn*[2] was dug
and a fire lit in it. Peeling onions and other vegetables and
cutting them into pieces of the right size followed, an exercise

---

2. An arrangement for cooking several dishes at once. A narrow, long
ditch is dug into the ground and firewood kept burning in it. Pots containing rice, lentils, etc. are placed over the length of the dahn to boil.

in which Madan frequently joined his father. Sardari Lal also made sweet and sour *ambal*[3] in a huge vessel—ambal being the favourite dish of the guests. Then he went on to boil rice in a huge brass cauldron. At just the right time, he would cover the vessel's mouth with a piece of canvas and turn it over to drain the excess rice water. This process ensured that the rice retained its form and flavour when served. A little miscalculation of time, and the rice would either turn soggy or get burnt. Sardari Lal had to be cautious in preparing food in weddings.

Around noon, the guests would sit in rows for the feast. They were first served boiled rice on the broad leaf platters placed before them. Men carrying buckets ladled out dal on the rice. Then came the servings of sweet boiled rice and leaf bowls of ambal.

When one lot of the guests had finished eating, it fell to Sardari Lal and Madan to pick up the leaf platters and leaf bowls and clean up the mess.

After all the guests had eaten and departed, Sardari Lal took his share from the food left in the vessels and distributed the rest to the other workers, who would each have brought a utensil in the hope of collecting leftovers.

Sardari Lal would then carry all the used vessels to the well. Drawing water from the well, he scrubbed and washed them till they shone. If the feast was held at night, and it was too late, Sardari Lal would do the cleaning the following morning.

Madan had a distinct memory of the wedding of Zaildar Dayaram's daughter. Workmen had gathered in the Zaildar's house many days before the ceremony. They had begun by

---

3. A sweet and sour delicacy made of pumpkin, which forms an important part of the Dogra cuisine.

spending whole days sprucing up the entire house. The whole building was whitewashed by men, while the womenfolk had given a fresh coat of parola to the stables and the cattle holds. Then for four whole days the women had sifted and winnowed heaps of rice and pulses. A day before the arrival of the bridegroom's party, arrangements were made for cots and bedding for the guests. Everyone was busy performing one chore or the other as if it were the wedding of their own sister or daughter.

On the wedding day, one man and one woman from each of the village families sent their representatives: a man and a woman to the zaildar's house to give a fitting welcome to the bridegroom and his party. The lane leading to the house was festooned with buntings of coloured paper.

When at last the marriage party had arrived in the evening, they were all there to receive it. The groom's people were invited to sit in rows for tea and snacks. After the tea, they were served food on leaf plates and when the guests got up after the meal, Sardari Lal and Madan collected the leftover sweets in a basket. Sardari Lal's wife had picked up the used leaf plates to throw them to the dung heap some distance away.

It was quite late by that time. Hastily, Sardari Lal bundled together *suchchis*[4] and boiled rice into his scarf. Putting dals and vegetable curries into the pot that he had brought from home, he lumped a portion of the leftover sweets in the other corner of his scarf, leaving the rest for his fellow workmen. Having finished the business of the day, Sardari Lal got up to leave. He held the pot of dal and vegetables and slung the scarf holding the dry food on his right shoulder. It was

4. A deep-fried version of roti, made from refined flour.

past midnight by then. Madan had fallen asleep on the bare ground in a corner of the house. Sardari Lal had called out to him in a low voice, 'Maddi, my son, get up. We have to go home now. It's already very late.'

Madan was after all just a small boy. Working the whole day long by his father's side had left him exhausted and he was now in deep slumber. Sardari Lal drew near him, held his hand and shook him gently. Madan woke up at last, and both father and son proceeded homewards, stumbling in the darkness.

Back at home, Madan's siblings were asleep, having waited too long. Mother shook them awake one by one and they sat down. To them, the potpourri of savouries was confusing in taste. But the children relished the oily suchchis. It was after a long time they had eaten such rich food. After finishing the meal, they had sweets. The rich food and sweets had made them forget how long they had waited for their meal.

The following day, the zaildar's newly wed daughter had left for her in-laws' home. Sardari Lal was one of the jheewars who had borne the bride's palanquin to the groom's place.[5] The in-laws had made a ritual gift of a live fowl to the palanquin bearers, flinging the bird around the palanquin in token of warding off the evil eye.

* * *

Madan was caught up in the web of those memories from morning till noon time. Gradually, afternoon gave way to evening and it was time for him to cast his fishing lines

---

5. Myth has it that Lord Rama Chandra, one of the incarnations of the Hindu God Vishnu, had miraculously created four jheewars to bear the palanquin of his bride, Sita. Ever since then, it had been the lot of jheewars to bear the bridal palanquins.

into the river. But Madan's mind was still weighed down by misgivings.

Used to living in dismal conditions as they were, Madan and Kanta had never thought that one day they would have a proper house of their own, a house safe from harsh weather and illumined by electric light. The government scheme had at least made both of them aware of their basic needs.

In the evening, Madan set out for the river as was his custom. He scratched the wet earth to extract worms, cut the creatures into pieces and put them on all the hooks on the line. Tying a big stone to one end of the line and a smaller one at the other, he fixed the tackles into the river.

The sun was setting. In the gathering darkness, the one idea that lit up Madan's mind was that relief was on its way to herald a bright future for his family. He had lost track of time. Later, lying in bed, the soothing thought lulled him to sleep.

A Hope Defeated

It was a Sunday morning. The sun had risen. Sweeping away darkness, its rays not only brightened up the prevailing grey-ness, but also rid the air of the chill, infusing it with warmth. The fields were lush with autumn crops. Melding with warm air, the dew on tree leaves and plants vapourized and rose to the sky.

Madan had got up as usual and brought home the fish caught on his lines placed in the river the previous night. He took a glass of water from the pitcher, poured into his palm, and splashed it on his face two or three times. Then he took a sip of water and gargled, and emptied the remaining water on his dust-laden hair. Putting down the empty glass, he tried to comb down his spiky hair with his fingers. In that biting cold, even a drop of water was like an electric shock.

Having washed his face, he bent low to enter his hut. His cotton kurta-pajama hung from a rope tied between the walls.

His teeth chattering with cold, he hastily covered his shivering body with the coarse cotton clothing. Then he held his light blanket, the loi, flapped it two or three times to rid it of any dust and vermin and wrapped it round himself.

Madan bent down again to step out of the hut and picking up the parcel of fish said to Kanta, 'Today, I will come back only after receiving the cheque from Mantriji. I might be late. Give the children whatever you have in the house. When I come back in the evening with the cheque, I'll bring eatables for both of us.'

Kanta brought a smile to her dry lips and replied reassuringly, 'You go on and don't worry. I'll manage.'

Madan gazed into Kanta's eyes and turned to go. Passing by the houses that stood on both sides of the village lanes, he thought that soon he too would have a house of own. He believed his wish was going to be fulfilled. That day his pace was more vigorous than usual. His feet walked the earth, but his mind galloped like Chetak[1] towards its goal.

His first halt was at Thoru's eatery. There he disposed of his fish for a hundred rupees and left without wasting a moment.

Then, instead of going to Desu Shah's shop as was his practice, he headed for the higher secondary school that was about three hundred metres away at one end of the bazaar. It hardly took him five minutes to reach the school gate.

The path leading to the school was festooned with colourful streamers. Welcome arches had been erected at two places with whole bales of cloth. The main gate of the school was decorated with a banana plant on each side supporting a banner atop them.

1. The warrior-king Maharana Pratap Singh's legendary horse.

The cleaning staff had done a fine job of sweeping the area. Lime had been sprinkled in the gutters on both sides of the bazaar. The place certainly looked like somebody as important as a minister was expected.

The crossroads and the main gate of the school were adorned with large pictures of the prime minister and other leaders. Little buntings of the ruling party fluttered in the breeze.

The police had erected a device at the school gate. All the visitors had to pass through this machine, after which, alert policemen frisked every person before allowing him to walk through the gate. A small canvas cabin had been erected on one side for screening women. The path leading to the policemen had been cordoned off with steel pipes.

Madan walked through this path and stood before the policemen. One of the policemen asked him to remove his loi. Following the instruction, Madan placed the loi on a steel pipe and presented himself again for frisking. The police-man, with a small hand-held gadget, scanned him from top to toe and then said, 'If you are carrying any cigarette matches, leave them here.'

'I quit smoking long ago,' Madan said with some pride, as he retrieved his loi from the steel pipe and crossed the gate to go towards the school ground.

The ground lay to the left of the school gate and opposite it was located the school office and classrooms. That day the school ground had been divided into many sections by steel pipes. A temporary pathway, guarded by steel pipes and decorated with the party buntings, led to the stage on the west side. The stage itself was done up with a beautiful carpet and a handsome awning. A carefully arranged lounge sofa and some chairs awaited the pleasure of important guests.

The pandal in front of the stage was divided into two equal parts, with mats spread on the ground, with one part reserved for men and the other for women. A few plastic chairs were also set on the right side, ostensibly for leaders and important party workers.

Loudspeakers had been installed strategically to broadcast the minister's voice in all directions.

The town had seldom seen such tight security arrangements. Men in uniform had been patrolling the bazaar since the morning. Constables from the local police station apart, police officers from the city could also be seen among them. Barbed wire separated the stage from the pandal.

It was about ten in the morning. Sunlight had raised the temperature to a comfortable level. Madan felt an upsurge of blood. He did not bother about the chill that still lingered in the shades. Early arrival had given him the advantage of sitting right in front of the stage. In fact, he was the first and only member of the audience present at that time.

A few children were playing in the pandal. Some organizers and labourers, hired for fixing the pipes and awnings, were wandering about here and there while a few others idled near the stage.

Madan felt contented in that he would be able to hear his name called from the stage and seated as he was, so close to the stage, it would not be difficult for him to go up to the stage and receive his cheque from the minister.

People began to drop in after some time and in a few moments the pandal was more than half full.

Meanwhile, the local block president, Pritam Singh, the contractor, Mukhtayar Singh, and the headman of Madan's village, Gulchain Singh, also arrived and took their seats on the stage along with some other members of the panchayat. Petty leaders began to speak.

Soon two buses stopped at the school gate. They were packed to capacity and some passengers were sitting on their roofs as well. They were all shouting slogans at the top of their voices, raising a great din. There was a moment's calm as the passengers alighted from the bus, waving small party flags.

About hundred and fifty of these men and women, both young and old, had got themselves frisked at the gate and reassembled inside. Then they formed themselves into a procession and marched to the pandal waving their little flags and shouting slogans. One among them would raise a slogan and the others responded to him with matching verve. On reaching the pandal, they sat down on the mats; the women, on the side meant for them, and the men on theirs.

The stage secretary stood up and whispered something to the man who was delivering a speech. The speaker handed over the microphone to the stage secretary and stood aside to let him speak instead.

As everyone fell silent in anticipation, the stage secretary made an announcement, 'Honourable Mantriji will arrive in five minutes.'

The audience became attentive. Those who were stepping out of the pandal returned to their seats. Others who were standing on the road outside the gate rushed to be checked before entry. Now everybody was in a hurry to reach the pandal.

It was about midday and quite warm in the bright sunlight. Madan's empty stomach had begun to rumble in protest. But today no hunger or thirst could bother him. He was as happy at the moment as a man in a bridegroom's party. Sky-high hopes of receiving a cheque for building a brick house had obliterated all his woes and wants.

Suddenly, everyone seated in the pandal began to look up. Madan also craned his neck to look skywards. A helicopter was flying in their direction from the east. An excited murmur rose in the pandal, 'Mantriji has come!'

The pandal crackled with excitement.

The helicopter drew nearer and headed towards the back of the pandal. At the back of the stage, on the other side of the boundary wall of the school, was situated the town's police station. The helicopter had landed on the sprawling ground in the front of it. A great commotion arose in the pandal as the engines of the helicopter were cut off. Standing on their toes, some people tried to have a look at it from above the wall. But they could hardly see anything since the helicopter had landed right behind the place where they were standing.

Presently, four or five white Ambassador cars and Gypsy jeeps approached the school gate. They all were stopped at the gate, except one white Ambassador, which was driven straight to the stage. Half a dozen police commandoes, who had come in a white Gypsy, ran alongside the car, providing it a moving cordon. The people who had alighted from other vehicles walked towards the stage.

The Ambassador came to a stop near the stage. It was imme-diately surrounded by gun-wielding commandoes. A constable opened the rear left door of the car and the minister stepped out. A large number of people bumbled about the car, mak-ing him invisible for a while.

The stage secretary began to raise slogans on the micro-phone. The audience responded with zeal and the pandal shook as everyone got up and began to shout slogans.

The minister advanced towards the stage and climbed the steps to the stage. The commandoes followed him closely, keeping him well covered. Then the other leaders ascended the stage. The tall, fair-skinned, and white-haired minister was a well-preserved man in his seventies. He was an imposing figure in his spotless white kurta-pajama and black leather shoes.

Turning towards the audience, the personage waved and the people went into another paroxysm of slogan shouting. The noise that followed was so loud that it was difficult to understand what the slogans were about.

The leaders on the stage now began to garland the minister and in a moment he was laden with flowers. A man stood on the stage plucking flowers and showering the minister and his supporters with petals. This spectacle went on for some ten minutes.

While the slogan shouting was going on, Madan had got up and managed to get closer to the minister. The great man appeared to him like a god who had descended from the sky. Pressing both palms together, he paid obeisance to him in the manner of a devotee before a temple deity.

After a while, the minister sat on the sofa, peeling off his garlands and placing them along with other flowers on a table placed before him.

The stage manager began to request the people politely, 'Please sit down, kindly do sit down where you are.'

After some time, the excited audience calmed down and took their places. Presently, it was time for speeches. The small-time leaders were the first to speak.

Mukhtyar Singh, the contractor, the president of the party's youth wing, began by raising slogans in favour of the minister and the audience responded enthusiastically. A robust and bearded man of thirty-five, he appeared to be a go-getter. Mukhtyar Singh now raised slogans in favour of the party and a group of young men standing at the back responded to him enthusiastically.

Then he spoke at length about the problems of the young people. Asserting that unemployment was the biggest problem of them all, he concluded his speech with a plea that the money the government spent on the development of the block should instead be used for removing unemployment, and that contracts for all the developmental projects should go to the party youth. The young men standing at the back of the pandal applauded thunderously and raised few more slogans.

'He wants to grab every contract for himself and corner all the developmental funds,' said a man sitting close to Madan, his mouth twisted in scorn.

Madan agreed mutely with his neighbour and turned his attention to the stage again.

Other leaders also voiced their own concerns and retreated from the microphone. Eventually, the minister himself was invited to speak. He got up from the sofa and waved to the audience once again as he approached the microphone. The people responded with a roar of approval.

The minister began his speech with words of praise for the local leaders. Madan was astonished. How could Mantriji have a good word for any of them, he wondered. The village headman Gulchain Singh had illegally grabbed government land adjoining the canal bank. He had even barricaded the path leading to the canal. Gulchain Singh did not permit anyone to win a contract for any government project in his village. He had built a culvert over the canal a year and a half ago, using very little cement in the construction. No wonder that the eight-inch high parapet on both sides of the bridge had crumbled away so soon! No less a ruffian himself, Mukhtyar Singh moved about with five goons.

There was not one among the leaders on the stage or those sitting there who deserved to be called a good man. Then why was the minister praising them? Madan Lal reasoned with himself that the high dignitary, poor innocent man that he was, had come from outside and must have been misled by the local leaders about Mukhtyar Singh and Gulchain Singh. He was not aware of the truth. Madan wondered why someone couldn't go up to the minister and tell him what the truth was.

Pulling himself out from the mesh of his thoughts, Madan diverted his attention once again to the minister's speech. '… Nobody here shall sleep hungry in our party's rule. No one shall remain homeless. The government will give money to every poor family to build a house. That is our minimum programme. That is our party's motto.' The audience greeted the minister's speech with some more slogans in his support and that of his party.

'Mantriji is God incarnate. He wants to give every poor family of this place a house to live in,' Madan thought. 'He is a nice man. He wishes everyone well. He wants to remove poverty from this country.' The minister had concluded his speech with '*Jai Hind*' and returned to the sofa amidst a thunderous applause.

The stage manager took the microphone again and after thanking the minister, made an announcement, 'Now the Honourable Minister will, with his own hands, give away cheques to fifteen families for building brick houses. Other families too will be receiving cheques after the meeting is over. Separate counters have been set up for each village. Those who do not receive their cheques here are requested to go to the classrooms after the meeting where these counters are being run.' Then the stage secretary began to read out the names on the list. 'Ram Rakkha,' he pronounced the first name.

Madan was all attention. Ram Rakkha rose and walked up to the stage. He lived in a village adjacent to Madan's.

The elderly man looked down and out in his shabby clothes. Walking slowly, he approached the minister and stood before him. The local leaders were also standing close by. The minister himself was standing in the midst of the leaders, facing the pandal. He had Ram Rakkha move close to him and then personally gave him a cheque. For a while, Ram Rakkha kept standing where he was. Photographers, who were waiting for the great moment at the foot of the stage, clicked their cameras. Barring one, they all had their shops in that bazaar itself. Madan knew they were there to take pictures for the newspapers.

'Suman Verma,' the stage secretary read out the second name from the list he held.

Suman Verma was a young woman of twenty-five. She wore a light green *salwar-kameez*. Her shoulder-length hair was tied up in a ponytail. A starched white dupatta was swathed modestly over her bosom and hung from her shoulders. With her left arm she held an eight-month-old baby to her bosom. Suman's husband had died seven months ago and the poor girl was a very young widow.

Suman Verma proceeded to climb to the stage as the elderly Ram Rakkha stepped down slowly from the other side. She stood close to the minister. The photographers again clicked their cameras while she accepted the cheque from the minister. After receiving the cheque and having her photograph taken with the minister, Suman Verma also stepped down.

Virumal came next. A resident of Madan's village, he used to work at Gulchain Singh's house. Hearing Virumal's name on the stage, Madan felt a rush of blood in his veins.

'Virumal is from my village. That means now they will begin calling out the names of other people from my village,' he thought. Squatting on the ground as he was, Madan stretched his legs and got ready to stand up. His loi had slipped from his shoulder. Madan straightened it and covered himself properly.

Virumal descended from the stage after receiving his cheque. The next name was called and it was not Madan's. All fifteen names were called and the respective fifteen people had gone up to the stage to receive their cheques from the minister. But his name was not called at all.

Madan had been waiting impatiently for his own name till the very last. The public meeting was about to end as the minister had handed over the cheque to the fifteenth person. All the people in the pandal were getting up, tired as they were of sitting on the ground for that long. The people at the back had already left the venue and reached the bazaar. A glow of satisfaction could be seen on the faces of the local leaders, since the public gathering they had organized for the minister was successful.

The villagers who had not received their cheques stood in the pandal, their eyes fixed on the stage with anticipation. The minister waved and proceeded to descend from the stage. All the leaders present on the stage followed him as one. Coming down the steps, the minister took leave of everyone and went towards his car. With great difficulty the minister's car wended its way through the crowd to the gate and turned towards the police station. People in the pandal also got up and began to move towards the school gate.

Arriving at the police station, the minister's car went straight to an awning where arrangements had been made for tea and snacks. A race to grab his attention followed. Local leaders, government officers, and party functionaries milled around to receive him, though they seemed more interested in drawing his attention to matters close to *their* hearts than showing him any genuine courtesy. Contractor Mukhtayar Singh and the Headman Gulchain Singh praised the Block Development Officer (BDO), pleading for cancellation of his transfer order. Likewise, others also made good use of the proximity the occasion had afforded them. The minister asked some of them to come to the city and accepted papers from others. After a cup of sugarless tea he bid everyone farewell again, and went towards the helicopter.

In a few moments, the helicopter engine made a huge noise as its blades began to rotate. Soon enough the machine was in the air raising a cloud of dust.

People standing on the ground waved bidding the minister farewell.

When the gathering had dispersed, Madan made his way through the crowd to the classrooms. There were some other people moving out of the crowd to go this way and that.

The counter for Madan's village was in the second room. He stood last in the queue to receive his cheque. In a few moments, many others came there to stand behind him.

Adjacent to the front wall of the room, a table of sorts had been made by joining two school desks. Behind this makeshift table were chairs on which sat the *gram sevak*—a village level functionary—and a clerk from the block development office to distribute cheques. The gram sevak asked the person's name and the clerk took out the beneficiary's cheque from a bundle. Then the beneficiary signed his name or left his thumb impression on a register and received the cheque.

When his turn came Madan spoke up. The clerk scanned the bundle of cheques, but did not find one in his name. He asked Madan to repeat his name and his father's.

'Madan Lal, son of Sardari Lal,' Madan said and looked at the clerk intently.

The clerk again scanned the cheques one by one once and then opened a file placed on the table. The file contained a three-page-long list of the beneficiaries. On carefully going through the file, he said to Madan, 'There's no cheque for you here.'

The clerk's words left Madan's face drained of blood. He felt the earth was slipping from under his feet. Neither his head nor heart was prepared to believe the official's words. Why was this man lying to him, he wondered.

The clerk motioned him to move aside. Madan moved aside but did not leave his place.

'Gram sevakji, my cheque has to be in this sheaf. Please look for it again. I too belong to the village for which you are giving away the cheques,' Madan said with folded hands.

Madan had taken advantage of his acquaintance with the village functionary not to leave his place. The familiarity had emboldened him further to make the request.

'We have run through the list twice before your eyes. The list is before you. You don't figure in it anywhere, nor is there any cheque for you,' the gram sevak replied, pointing at the sheaf of the cheques as well as the file.

Madan stood like a statue.

'You better go to the last room. The BDO is there. Take your chance, speak to him,' said the gram sevak, closing the file and putting it back on the table.

Madan had clearly heard the announcement made on the stage that the counters were being run village-wise. He could not understand why his cheque was not there. Why had his name been left out? This counter was meant for his village. The men who had been standing ahead of him and even those behind him were from his village. They had all got their cheques. How could it be that his name did not exist in the counter for his own village?

Pestered by such questions, Madan left the queue, allowing the man behind him to take his place.

He moved towards the last room in the row where the BDO was to arrive. The peon standing at the door said that the officer had gone to the police station to oversee the arrangements for serving tea and snacks to the minister and his entourage. He would arrive there only after the minister had left.

For Madan, there was nothing else to do but wait for the BDO. It was the question of the fulfilment of his life's desire. It was the question of the happiness of his family. It was the question of finding a refuge from the chill of winter and heat of the summer. And it was a question of his elevation in the community as an owner of a brick house. Now, as before, everyone would keep calling him 'Madan, the shanty-man'. He had been deprived of the opportunity to be the owner of a brick house and be counted among house owners in the village. Madan's train of thoughts trundled on without halt. He was perturbed.

Madan stood waiting outside the BDO's room. Turning aside, he saw that, one by one, the officials who had been distributing money had left. That confused him. He passed some more time in this manner. Impatient with the unending wait, he asked himself, 'Why shouldn't I go myself to the other counters and make enquiries?' His feet, of their own accord, took him towards the other counters.

At the first counter, Madan stood once again at the end of the queue. The man who ran the counter was another clerk from the block development office and was known to him. Filled with hope, Madan advanced to the counter on his turn.

'Madan, please go to the counter of your own village in the next room. You are not listed here ...,' the clerk said without examining the sheaf of cheques. 'This counter is for other people,' the man added, finishing his incomplete sentence.

Confused, Madan left that counter and went to the third one. That counter was managed by two persons—Pradip Sharma, the *patwari*[2] from his village, and a functionary who belonged to another office. Once again Madan stood at the end of the queue. When at last his turn came, there was not a single man standing behind him.

'Why have you come to this centre? The counter for *your* village is in the back room,' Pradip Sharma said, on recognizing him.

Madan stood deferentially before the patwari, bidding him namaste. Having waited for the village revenue official to finish, he proceeded to say, 'The village counter does not have my cheque ...' Madan swallowed hard to continue, 'My name does not exist even in that three-page list. I've come to this counter to see if, by mistake, my cheque might be here.' Choking with emotion, Madan spoke with difficulty.

The other official with Patwari Pradip Sharma was winding up for the day. He collected the file, counter-foils of the cheques issued, and sundry other papers on the table. Both men were preparing to go home. Getting up from his

2. Village-level revenue official.

chair behind the table, Pradip Sharma said to Madan in a level voice, 'Cheques have been made out only in favour of persons whose names figure in the list. There is no cheque for anyone else.'

Madan felt his boat was sinking in deep waters. He said in a very low voice, 'But my name does not exist in the village list.'

Patwari Pradip Sharma came forward from behind the table and moving towards the door, said, 'Madan, if your name is not in the list, you won't be given a cheque.'

Walking out of the room, the patwari went towards the last room in which the BDO was sitting. The clerk followed the Patwari, carrying all his papers with him.

Madan felt numb—all the vitality seeped out of his body. The shock of being told that he would not be getting a cheque for a brick house had hit him like an electric current. It took him some minutes to get a grip on himself.

'How can that be?' He asked himself. 'It was only a while ago that Mantriji declared that no one in his regime would live without a brick house, that all those families who live in mud houses would be given money to build pukka houses. I am poorer than the poorest. I live in a hut. My hut is worse than a mud house.'

Mustering courage, Madan walked swiftly to catch up with Pradip Sharma and trying to keep pace with him, he said, 'Patwari Sahib, how can it be? I enrolled myself with the Village Council and they knew very well that I live in a thatched hut. Patwari Sahib, you know too well that I am a poor man, with small children to raise.'

Patwari Pradip Sharma listened to Madan while they walked together. But the petty revenue official could not perceive the heartache which Madan felt on seeing the castles of his hopes crumble before his eyes. Listlessly, he reached for the door leading to the room of the BDO.

The recipients of the cheques had left. Now only government officials could be seen going about the place.

Before entering his superior's room, Patwari Pradip Sharma stopped at the door and said to Madan in a bland tone, 'Look, Maddi, it is too late now. We all had a busy day today because of the minister's visit. I am very tired. Besides, I have had nothing to eat since morning. I am famished. What you should do is to come tomorrow and make your enquiries.' But Madan did not seem to hear the patwari and continued to stand behind him.

Folding his hands and dropping his head slightly forward, the patwari bade namaste to the man sitting in the room behind a table facing the door. Momentarily, he barred Madan's entry.

But there was nothing that could stop Madan today. Dejected though he was, the memory of the minister's declaration had kept a ray of hope burning in him. The sight of the high official aroused a new eagerness in him. Madan was not yet ready to abandon hope altogether.

He willed himself to follow Pradip Sharma into the room. Employees from nearly all counters were depositing their registers, files, and other papers into the boxes placed in the room. Some of them sat on chairs lining three sides of the room. There was not a single vacant chair.

Noticing Pradip Sharma paying his respects, Madan understood that the forty-five-year-old moustached man, with deep small-pox marks on his cheeks and forehead, was the BDO himself. Madan also folded his hands, dropped his head slightly forward, and said namaste to the authority.

The BDO acknowledged Madan's courtesy with a nod and asked him the purpose of his visit.

At the officer's question a hundred wishes stormed through Madan's mind: a rise in his standing in the community as the owner of a pukka house; an electrified room and his children studying deep into the night in the glow of an electric bulb; the end of the draughty winter; the end, too, of summer dust storms; and, the luxury of living in a dry room during the monsoon. He felt an insuperable compulsion to secure a cheque from the officer even though the subordinate officials had told him many times that he would not be getting anything of the sort. So strong was Madan's urge for the cheque that his mouth refused to utter a word.

It was Pradip Sharma who told the BDO about Madan and why he had not been issued a cheque.

Madan kept standing before the BDO in his humble posture. When Pradip Sharma had finished, he managed to say in a quivering voice, 'I live in a saroot-thatched hut in the village. I am the poorest of the poor, yet I didn't get a cheque for building a brick house …'

The officials seated all around that room seemed to be in a hurry. The BDO, Patwari Pradip Sharma, and the clerks thought they were done with their day's duties. They were now thinking of closing down for an early return to their homes. To them Madan's visit was an unwarranted brake on their departure. Languidly, they heard what Madan had to say to the BDO.

'Under the scheme of providing funds for construction of pukka houses, only the families that figure in the list have been issued cheques …' The BDO tried to explain to Madan.

'Madan's name does not exist in the list, sir,' interjected the gram sevak in the hope that Madan would go away on hearing that the matter had been closed once for all. Clarifying what the gram sevak had said, the BDO added, 'That is why you are not getting a cheque under the scheme.'

But Madan did not budge from that place. His face still wore a pleading look.

'It's too late today. We have packed away all the documents. You may come tomorrow and enquire if you wish,' the BDO said at last, dismissing him from his office for the day.

The BDO had no idea that what he considered an insignificant part of his job meant so much in Madan's life. To him a name in a list was just a name, the list itself nothing more than a piece of paper on which some names have been inscribed in black ink. Little did the BDO care that behind a three-syllable name was a whole family compelled to live a life of poverty and dire need.

The BDO failed to understand how deeply he had hurt Madan's feelings by his cold responses to a poor man's feverish entreaties. To him the cheque barely amounted to his own salary for two months and to Madan it meant the fulfilment of his fondest dream. The BDO could merrily spend the cheque amount in just a couple of months. But for Madan that amount was sufficient to enable him realize his life's hopes. It meant an end of most of the problems that beleaguered him.

The BDO and the men in his staff were hungry and a hearty meal was their first priority. All they wanted was to pack up their papers and go somewhere to eat. The BDO had arranged a lunch for them at government's expense.

Madan was sinking into despondency. The BDO was the highest authority. He had personally told Madan that no cheque would be issued to him. Whatever was to happen would happen on the morrow. Madan decided it was no use staying there any longer and that he should return home.

With a fallen face he folded his hands once again, bowed his head slightly forward and bidding namaste to the BDO, turned away and left the room. On an empty stomach since the morning, he was drained of energy, his own body a burden to carry.

Coming back from the block development office, Madan went through the verandah towards the playground. Two hours ago, there had been a huge gathering there and much bustle, but now the venue was almost empty. Mats covering the ground had mostly been wrapped up and loaded onto a mini truck, though a few still lay spread on the ground. Two boys were busy untying the ropes to bring down an awning. A couple of policemen in mufti had wound up the barbed wire fence that had been installed in front of the stage and were carrying it back to the police station. Men from the water supply department were dismantling the barricade on the ground and carrying the steel pipes to load it into a blue government truck stationed outside the school premises. The buntings on the ropes fluttered idly in the wind. The school ground was littered with torn pieces of multicoloured plastic buntings of the party.

The police detail on the main gate had left and the school looked deserted.

To Madan everything seemed empty. He did not want to look at anything. He did not want to talk to anybody. The question that pestered his mind constantly was why his name didn't figure in his village list. He had himself got his name registered with the Village Council. Why had his name been dropped *after* its inclusion in the list? It was not as if it had been an oversight. He had no quarrel with anyone in the village. He did not annoy anyone. If he happened to come across even a lad of the zamindar class, he would humbly say namaste to him. He made it a point to say namaste to every member of the Village Council. He was also equally respectful to the government functionaries.

Engaged in these thoughts, Madan passed through the bazaar and reached Desu Shah's shop. He climbed the two steps into the shop and sat on the bench inside.

Desu Shah sat close to his chest, sipping his evening tea from a stainless steel tumbler brought from his home. Sitting on a bench, his son, Sohan, was also sipping tea from a stainless steel tumbler. Seeing Madan approach the shop, Sohan drained his tea quickly and placed the empty glass on the bench near Desu Shah.

On Madan's asking, Sohan weighed flour and other things on the balance and put them into paper bags. Madan paid in cash, and wending his way through the bazaar, took the path to his village.

Madan was still sunk in dejected thoughts. If only the BDO had inscribed just one more name in the list, he too would have figured there. It would have taken that man no more than five minutes, but Madan would have got funds to build himself a brick house to last a lifetime.

The day was a Sunday. There were no school children going that way. The sun was losing its warmth, there was a chill in the air, and the cold wind of a winter evening had begun to blow.

Wheat growing on both the sides of the path waved gently in the air. The fluttering leaves looked pretty. In the rows of the wheat crops extending far into distance, the mustard plants stood taller than the other crops.

There was a time when Madan used to feel happy walking through these fields. But that day nothing seemed to please him. His eyes fixed to the ground, he walked the trodden path like a robot without caring to look at anything around him.

'The government wants to do so much for the poor. Mantriji said in his speech today that no one in his regime would go hungry, no one would live in a mud house. But when my luck is bad, how can I blame anyone?' Madan muttered to himself. 'I wonder what bad deeds I might have committed in my previous birth that god is annoyed with me. One gets only what He bestows. My family will build a pukka house when He builds us one.'

The strands of thought took him back to a year and half ago when people in the village said that the government had announced a scheme for the poor and the unemployed. Madan had owned neither a radio, nor a television set. His knowledge was limited to what he heard from the village folk.

Much Smoke and No Fire

Summer was at its peak. It was about five in the evening and Madan had been resting in the shade of some mango trees for more than three hours to escape from the seething heat. He had removed his shirt and placed it in a corner. His ribs could easily be counted, sticking out as they were from the dark and parched skin of his chest and back. His stomach was a cave under his rib cage. A few other emaciated villagers, daily wagers like Madan, were also seated on the ground beside him. Present too were three or four school dropouts.

Then there was the barber, Sardara, who plied his trade from that very place. Sardara took keen interest in village matters and government policies and was fond of listening to newscasts. Even though other people had acquired television sets, Sardara still carried an antiquated Philips transistor radio which he pressed to his ears throughout the day.

Madan, who sat near him, listened attentively. It was something about a government scheme to provide jobs to people in villages.

'If I wanted a job, would I get one?' asked Chaman Lal.

Chaman, too, was from Madan's village and was about his age. A hard worker, he laboured sincerely as a daily wager.

'Why not? The benefit is meant for all India's villagers,' Sardara replied to Chaman.

'What would I have to do for this?' Chaman Lal pressed Sardara for answer to another question.

'That I don't know. What I heard over the radio, I've shared with you,' Sardara replied.

Madan felt that the government scheme was meant for people who had no regular job and that he too should benefit from it. He returned home with that thought. Later, as was his habit, he went to his cousin, Tarsem, to gather more details.

Reaching Tarsem's house late in the evening, he sat on a cot and asked him, 'Is it true that the government has floated a scheme to provide work to whosoever might want it in villages?'

'Yes, that's true,' Tarsem replied.

'What will I have to do for this? How will government give me work?'

'You should go to the BDO to have your name registered with his office. Work will be given only to those who are registered. The scheme is called "NREGA", the National Rural Employment Guarantee Act.'

'Tell me in plain words what all it means.'

'It means that the government will give work to unemployed village people.'

'I don't know much beyond what I have told you,' added Tarsem. 'I will go tomorrow to the office of the BDO to get more details. Then I'll be able to brief you fully.'

Tarsem's mother brought them tea in glass tumblers. Madan got up and bowed to touch his *chachi*'s feet before taking a tumbler for himself. He returned to the cot and sat with Tarsem drinking tea. On his way back home, the delightful taste of the tea he had had with his cousin lingered, though with a suppressed feeling of guilt that while he had enjoyed the pleasure of an evening tea, his wife and children hadn't had anything of the sort.

True to his word, Tarsem got all the details from the BDO's office the following day and went to Madan's home in the evening. Both Kanta and Madan were home. Kanta was making rotis in the tuala. Madan, wielding an axe, was chopping driftwood that he had brought from the river, so it could be used as fuel for the chulha. The summer day's hard work had brought sweat to his face, as to the rest of his body.

On seeing Tarsem, Madan stopped chopping wood. Putting his axe aside, he drew near his cousin and bade him namaste with a smile. Tarsem extended his right hand and Madan placed both his hands on it. Both the men walked towards the mud-plastered compound. Madan asked Tarsem to wait while he rushed inside the hut and brought back a cot and his loi. He spread the cot and covering it with the loi, motioned to Tarsem to sit on it.

Sitting comfortably on the cot, Tarsem asked after his health and about the children, 'How are Kamal and Kamlesh getting on with their studies?'

'They are doing well. Both of them go to school.'

'I don't see Usha and Louku. Where are they?' Tarsem was going to say something looking in the direction of the hut when Kanta brought water in brass tumblers. Tarsem accepted a tumbler from Kanta's hands and began to sip.

'Usha and Louku may have gone out to play,' Madan replied to Tarsem. Then he told Kanta that he was going to fetch milk in a glass and that she should, in the meanwhile, put tea on the chulha to boil.

'No, no, I won't have tea,' Tarsem insisted. Getting up, he caught Madan by the arm and made him sit again on the cot. Tarsem knew how difficult it was to get milk at that time of the day, and he did not want poor Madan to go to any unnecessary expense.

Getting down to business, Tarsem told him that the government had charted out a scheme for the whole country. NREGA applied to all those physically able villagers who wanted to work and can earn a living, but had no gainful employment in the village.

'But what exactly do *we* get out of it?' Madan probed deeper.

'Under the scheme, the government guarantees employment for at least a hundred days in a year. That means it will pay wages for a hundred days a year to each of the registered persons,' Tarsem tried to explain.

'The government will pay wages for a hundred days in a year even if it does not hire a man that long!' Madan repeated in his mind. Happy at the idea, he asked, 'What will I have to do to benefit from this scheme? Who will allot work to me? Where will the government send me to work?'

'Any man in the village who wants to work under the scheme will have to enlist with the BDO's office. The enlisted man would be employed on the development jobs in his own village. Such jobs could be things like building roads to connect one village with another, laying gutters and lanes within the village, digging channels to carry water for irrigation, constructing small overpasses on the channels, and so forth,' Tarsem said.

Madan thought it sounded too good to be true. In order to remove the last trace of doubt, he remarked, 'If the government does not get these jobs done, then neither does a man get wages for a hundred days!'

'But that is the guarantee, brother. Even if the government does not actually put the enlisted men to work, it stands to pay wages for a 100 days a year to each and every one of them,' Tarsem emphasized.

Madan thought happily, 'We people keep wandering here and there in search of work. If a mate[1] does get me work, I have to pay him ten rupees out of a day's wage of one hundred, and for nothing. Now it would be much easier for me to find work. I will save the ten rupee commission and not be obliged to the mate either. And best of all is that even if the government has no work to offer, I will still pocket a full hundred days' wages.'

'I am thinking of going to the BDO's office tomorrow to get myself registered,' Madan broke his silence.

'The scheme will commence in our district from the first of the next month. Each one of the enlisted persons will be given a job card. This way he will be able to keep an account of the work done by him during the year.'

Madan was determined to work under NREGA. As Tarsem got up to leave for his home, Kanta and Madan wished they could invite him for supper that evening. Kamla got up from inside the tuala and said to him, 'Please stay with us for supper. It will be ready in no time.'

---

1. A man hired by a contractor to supervise labour.

'I'll eat with you some other day.' Saying this, Tarsem made to leave. Madan did not force him since he knew that for the night they had nothing but water and one or two potatoes boiled with a whole lot of salt.

'You could have eaten one or two rotis with us,' Kanta said again to Tarsem, who was leaving now. Tarsem excused himself and set out in the direction of his home. Madan walked with him for some distance to see him off. Coming back, he sat down on his cot and Kanta went back to her chores.

After a while, Madan picked up his axe and began to chop wood.

* * *

The month came to an end, and then it was the first of the next month. Madan reached the BDO's office just as its doors opened. The BDO arrived half an hour later as several people stood waiting outside his office.

Mukhtyar Singh too was there, holding a long list of names. The BDO read aloud all those names in Madan's presence. These were the names of the roughnecks that Mukhtyar Singh always kept in his retinue. Madan was puzzled as to why those fellows would toil on the daily wage of a hundred rupees. In a day, he reckoned, each one of Mukhtyar Singh's boys spent more than that trailing Mukhtayar Singh on his bike. In the evening he wasted yet another hundred or more on hooch alone. Not less than fifty rupees did he burn on cigarettes. Would such wastrels be prepared to lift baskets of sand and rubble with him? Would they sweat it out in the scorching heat of a summer day? Madan found no answer to his questions. He was left to ask himself again and again, 'How can it be?'

The village headman too was there. He also gave a list to the BDO—a list of his men.

Likewise, workers of some other political parties had also arrived to have their men registered.

Madan knew most of the men. Barring a few who had worked with him on daily wages, he doubted whether others would deign to work as common labourers. Their interest in the scheme lay only in becoming 'regular' daily wage-earners, he thought. The department of canals also employed daily wagers who after a spell were given permanent government jobs. If that happened, Madan thought, he too would be entitled to a pension. The opportunity would transform his life beyond his wildest dreams and resolve all his difficulties.

Madan got his name registered. The official responsible for the registration knew him. When the process was over, he said to Madan, 'Maddi, you may collect your job card after twelve days and then keep visiting us personally till you get some work.'

In a couple of days it came to be known that the Minister for Rural Development was visiting the town to inaugurate the scheme.

The minister as well as the local MLA arrived on the appointed date. The department of rural development had made elaborate arrangements for their welcome and there was a sizeable crowd. Many people had gathered. The minister himself gave away a few job cards from the stage and the remaining cards were issued by the BDO's office.

The programme went on till the evening. The minister made a speech. He told the audience about the NREGA scheme and the benefits it would bring to the villagers. The enlisted men collected their job cards and went home.

Work began in three weeks' time. It was a NREGA project of laying the street outside the residence of the village headman, Gulchain Singh, who himself was the contractor.

Gulchain Singh was accustomed to cornering all the contracts for any village development project and the officials in the department feared him. If a contract was given to anyone else, the chances were either that the work would not be completed, or even if it was completed somehow, there would be complaints against them.

From a message sent by the gram sevak Madan came to know that the NREGA work had begun. At that time he was working as a labourer with the mason, Manga, on raising the boundary wall of someone's house. He spoke to the mason about his preference for the NREGA work and collected his wages in full.

The following day he reached outside Gulchain Singh's house where the work was to begin. He sweated it out till the evening. On finishing the day's work, he washed the mortar basin and the spade before putting them aside. Washing his face, hands, and feet, he prepared to go home with some others. Then came the moment to receive some money for the day's expenses. Madan joined the queue of labourers waiting for the mate.

The mate, who also entered, announced tersely, 'Earlier I used to pay you a day's wages in full or expenses for the day, but now under this scheme, I can pay you nothing in cash.'

'Why so? Has your treasury gone empty?' mocked Jamit Raj, who also belonged to the village. He often joined Madan to work for daily wages. Jamit Raj had a rough sense of humour and was wont to joke with everyone, keeping the atmosphere light.

'Our treasury cannot go empty so soon. But men who work under this scheme get their wages directly from the block development office. That too not in cash but through cheques,' said the mate in reply to Jamit Raj.

The laughing men fell silent. The officious manner of presenting the facts had robbed them of mirth.

'Why from the BDO's office? We are working for you,' countered Jamit Raj. His tone had changed.

'Both the gram sevak and the contactor, Gulchain Singh have told me that the payment for fifteen days' wages will be made by the BDO's office through cheques which you can encash at your bank any day within six months' time,' said Rashpal to the assembled labourers. 'And one more thing,' he added after a meaningful pause, 'you will receive seventy rupees a day.'

There was a terrible silence. They were anxious to know whether he was telling them the truth.

'Only seventy rupees?' Jamit Raj enquired anxiously. 'But we signed up for a hundred rupees a day!' The others were also perplexed. With sad eyes and glum faces they sought an answer from Rashpal.

'You will get what the government pays you. Not a paisa more!' The mate replied crossly. But he lowered his voice immediately and said, 'Government has fixed a day's wage at seventy rupees. No labourer can be paid more than that. In the NREGA scheme, payments are made through cheques issued in the names of men who actually show up for work. There is no way we can fake more labourers and draw excess money to pay you a hundred rupees a day.'

The men had grown pensive. As far as they could remember, such a thing had never happened before. Work by the day and wages in the evening—that had been their routine. If it was not the whole wage, then a part of it to meet their immediate expenses, and the balance paid in two or three days.

'We have worked at various government projects till now, but nowhere were we paid what you call 'the government rate'.

If indeed it is that, then how could *they* pay us more?' Jamit Raj mumbled, as he proceeded towards his home.

Madan was also perturbed. He was used to taking his wages home every evening to buy rations and other things. It was what kept his hearth warm. Here too they should have had some sort of a system for providing a minimum payment to workers every day. But Rashpal had bluntly refused to give them anything. To top it, he had said that nothing would be paid before fifteen days. And then a direct cut of thirty rupees in a day's wage!

Madan had nothing to take home to his hungry wife and children. That was his immediate concern. In that predicament, he thought of his messiah of difficult times.

The other workers had set out for their homes, but Madan went instead to Mason Manga's house.

Manga Mistri's house was located on the roadside. Men and beasts crossed this end of the road throughout the day. Animals would stray into the house if the front door was left open. To prevent this, Manga had erected a steel gate which was usually closed. Madan knocked at the door.

'Come, Madan, do come in,' Manga said on seeing Madan. 'I too have reached home only now.'

Clad in tailor-made *kachha*[2] and a vest, Manga Mistri came to the gate to receive Madan.

'*Mistriji*,[3] pardon me, but I won't come in. I have to tell you something here itself,' said Madan. He did not want to say anything before Manga's wife and children. 'Today I didn't get my wages,' he said, 'and there's not a paisa in my pocket. I am in dire need of fifty rupees.'

2. Indian-style men's underwear—loose, thigh-length shorts.
3. Mistri is a generic term for artisans. Here it means 'mason'.

Leaving Madan at the gate, Manga went indoors, fetched a fifty-rupee note in his closed fist and gave it to Madan. He knew that though Madan was poor, he made it a point to clear his debts.

'Mistriji, I want to return to work with you from tomorrow,' Madan said beseechingly.

'That would be fine. Come tomorrow,' said Manga after a brief pause.

Madan bade him namaste and coming out of the gate, went towards the shop to buy rations.

That night Madan kept thinking. It would not be possible for him to work under the government scheme for all of fifteen days. The daily wage would be seventy rupees instead of one hundred, which meant a loss of thirty rupees. It was not a profitable proposition at all.

'The decision I have taken to go back to work with Manga Mistri is right after all,' concluded Madan as he fell asleep.

From the next day Madan began to work again with Mason Manga at some other house in the village.

After a lapse of fifteen days he got a message from the BDO's office to collect his wages.

Madan went to the BDO's office and received his cheque of seventy rupees. The clerk there told him that he would get seventy rupees in cash on presenting the cheque in any branch of the Jammu & Kashmir Bank. Madan went to the nearest branch of the bank. On his turn in the queue, he handed over the cheque to the bank clerk.

'Deposit it into your account. Otherwise—no cash for you,' the clerk said.

'But I don't have an account with the bank,' Madan replied to the clerk.

'You see, it's an "account payee" cheque, which means it has to be deposited into an account. If you don't have any account with us, then open one,' the bank clerk said while returning the cheque to Madan. In the meanwhile, another customer handed over his cheque to the clerk.

Madan approached another official of the bank for opening his account and was given instructions. He would have to present two passport-size photos of his own and deposit at least five hundred rupees to open an account. The photos alone would cost him forty rupees.

Astounded, Madan went to the manager's room with the cheque and implored him to give him seventy rupees against the cheque. But the manager sent him away empty-handed.

Madan came to despise the government scheme of NREGA. Carrying the seventy-rupee cheque like a piece of paper, he came out of the bank and went home. He kept the cheque in safe custody in the hope that someday he might receive the amount that it promised him.

The Blackest is Grey

That day Madan returned home after facing yet another
letdown. He could see nothing ahead but abject poverty and
helplessness. No ray of hope shone for him.

From the street came the sound of children at play.
Oblivious to the noise and lost in his thoughts, Madan stood
before his hut. As he stared at it regretfully, he knew that the
worn shanty would forever be his home.

His children were playing in the street along with other
children. They would return home only after sunset, when
their bellies began to hurt.

Kanta sat before a fire in her tuala. Big dreams swam in
her eyes and she was very happy. On seeing Madan, she got
up enthusiastically. Coming out of the tuala, she greeted him
with a faint smile and extending her hand, took the paper bag
of rations from him. Madan let go the bag into her grip and

withdrew his hand. Kanta went back into the tuala and put the bag where she had been sitting.

Madan did not return Kanta's smile. He followed her sadly into the tuala and sat beside her without a word.

Looking at Madan's morose expression, Kanta thought he might be tired and hungry as he had eaten nothing since morning. She took out a clean brass tumbler from a basket made of mulberry branches. Going to the pitcher rack outside the tuala, she filled it with water and gave it to Madan and got busy taking things out of the paper bag.

It was winter and the water was very cold. Madan finished the glass in just two gulps.

Kanta got up again, went to the door and bending down, entered the hut. She came back quickly with an aluminium basin, a round sieve to sift flour, some water in a jug and sat down again at her place in the tuala. Sifting the flour and mixing it with water, she began to knead the dough.

'When did Mantriji go back?' Kanta asked Madan.

Madan was weak with hunger and sorrow had silenced him. He said nothing.

Kanta looked intently at Madan and realized that he was not only tired but dejected as well. She paused in her kneading and asked him, 'What's the matter with you? Unwell?'

Madan discarded his hunched position and looking directly at Kanta, said, 'I am well. But what has been done to us today is not well.'

Kanta stopped kneading altogether—like some electric machine coming to a stop. She could not understand what had happened. Words tumbled from her mouth of their own accord, 'Didn't you go to collect the cheque? Where's the cheque that we were to get under the government scheme to build our brick house?'

Madan sighed and said in a low tone, 'We didn't get it, Kanta.'

He told her the whole story of the day. Stunned, as if electrocuted, and her ashen face sagging, Kanta listened to him lifelessly.

It was not the first time in her life that Kanta had faced disillusionment. Countless desires had she nursed since childhood. She had wanted to gorge on the choicest sweets. Wear the finest dresses. Adorn herself with jewels. Buy goodies for her children. But she had to suppress her desires over and over again. On every such occasion she had to reason with herself that such things were not for her. That day had brought her even more disillusionment, only it was more shattering than anything else in her past.

Kanta took time to come out of her despair. To her it was like waking up from a sweet dream—from fantasy—to the stark reality of life.

Reverting to her routine, Kanta resumed her cooking and in a short while was putting hot rotis on Madan's plate. Food revived Madan. He began to worry about where he would get money to buy rice, flour, and other groceries, the following day.

Madan always ate after his children had eaten. But that day he could not wait because he was hungrier than usual and also had to go to the river to fix the tackles. He was already late for the job. Worried lest the children went short of food, Madan stopped eating and rose, his stomach only half full. He would eat on his return from the river if there was anything left, he decided.

He took hold of his tackle and set out for the river. By that time everyone else had left the river front. The path was empty. The proximity of the river had caused faint beads of dew to appear on tiny leaves of grass even at that time of the evening.

On reaching the river bank, Madan detached the barbs on the lines. Extracting worms from his usual place, he cut them into pieces and put the bait on each barb before flinging the line into the river with a heavy stone tied to one end. He put two more large stones on it to ensure that any big fish caught on the barb could not carry the tackle away. The sun was setting and a fog rose from the cold river.

He came back to the village late in the evening, when the sunlight had dipped completely. The streetlights looked brighter in the dark as Madan advanced towards the village, his mind working all the time. Approaching the village limits, Madan turned to another lane rather than going to his own home—the lane that led to Tarsem's home.

Madan still could not bring himself to believe that he was not going to receive the cheque to build his own brick house. He just could not accept the bleak truth, since he had himself registered his name with the Village Council.

* * *

Tarsem's father, Shailo Ram, and Madan's father, Sardari Lal, had the same paternal grandfather. They were very close and the first to reach out to each other in an hour of need.

Withstanding all life's troubles and travails without letting out a sigh, Shailo Ram had seen his son Tarsem through a master's degree. He felt proud of his son's academic achievements. Shailo Ram was not very old, but perhaps because of poor diet and labour harder than his body could stand, he had aged rapidly. There was hardly any flesh between his dark skin and skeleton, his hair was grey, and the beard on his dark face had turned completely white.

Tarsem was a slim youth of medium height. One of the best swimmers of his age in the river Chenab region, he was equally good at studies. After a master's degree in Economics, he had found the job he wanted, that of a teacher at a senior secondary school. But even during his student days he had taken private jobs to supplement his family's meager income.

Tarsem's handsome salary had improved the condition of Shailo Ram's house in a matter of two-three years. At least, they did not have to worry about their evening meal anymore. Tarsem had got married the previous year and built himself a brick-and-mortar room. And there was also electricity in the house.

Immensely proud of his son's brick house though Shailo Ram was, he still preferred to sleep in his old hut.

In the grey light of the dusk, from inside his room, Tarsem saw Madan approaching. Madan walked straight to him into the room. Shailo Ram was also there. Bowing to touch his uncle's feet, Madan said, '*Chachu, perain pauna!*'[1]

'May you live long, my son,' said Shailo Ram, blessing Madan.

Then Madan shook Tarsem's hand and sat down by his uncle's side.

He told Tarsem that he had not received the cheque since his name was not in the list of beneficiaries. Narrating the whole day's story to him, he sought Tarsem's validation, 'You were also there when I registered with the Village Council. Weren't you?'

Tarsem nodded in affirmation. He was listening attentively to Madan, whose face was charged with deep anguish.

Going on with his tale of woe, Madan added, 'Biroomal and Ram Krishan, the priest have got their cheques. But there was no cheque for me.'

---

1 I bow to your feet, uncle!

'God too is partial to the rich. They who have everything are given more, and the needy get nothing until He's pleased,' Shailo Ram remarked.

Showing no response to his father's remark, Tarsem said, 'There's no doubt that you did register with the Village Council, but at the end of the day, it is the BDO who has to attest any list submitted to him on behalf of the Village Council ...'

Madan interrupted Tarsem before he could finish, 'Can there be any doubt that I live in a hut? You tell me, is there a poorer man in the village? Anyone can see that I am the poorest man here.'

In the glow of the electric bulb hanging from the ceiling of his room, Tarsem could read the expression of utter misery on the withered face of the man who claimed he was the poorest man in the village. Conceding the assertion, Tarsem began to explain, 'Look, the BDO's attestation is required to ensure that the claim meets all the conditions laid down by the government, such as proof of residence, your ration card and the patwari's evidence.'

Madan listened to Tarsem attentively. Shailo Ram was also paying close attention to the talk between the two. He felt proud that his son had such a deep understanding of the matter. Was he not better educated than anyone else? Not only in his immediate family but among all his relatives?

Tarsem finished with an assurance to Madan that he would be on leave the following day—a Monday—and would accompany him to the BDO's office to gather more information.

A footfall at the doorstep diverted their attention. Tarsem's mother had come in carrying two platefuls of food. Without getting up, Madan said, 'Perain pauna, chachi.'

'Live long, my son,' blessed the aunt, placing one plate before Shailo Ram and the other before Madan.

'I eaten before going to the river. Please give it to Tarsem,' Madan said to his chachi.

'One round to the river and back and you'd be hungry again. You must eat now,' Shailo Ram told Madan.

During this exchange, Tarsem had taken the plate from his mother's hand and offered it to Madan. Madan accepted the plate without a word.

After a bellyful of food which was much tastier than what he usually ate at home, Madan rinsed his mouth. He sat there a bit longer and sought leave of Shailo Ram and Tarsem to go home.

It was about 8.30 on a wintry night. Most people were home. The odd dog barked in the street, while its companions lay asleep, their noses tucked into their tails. Houses shone with electric lights. Water overflowing from drains had made the ground slushy. Disjointed voices emanated from a few houses. But it was largely quiet, with the residents lying wrapped up in cosy quilts inside their homes.

From beyond the village, could be heard the sound of an approaching tractor. It was the village headman coming home.

Generally people in the villages did not turn off their lights since there were no meters to gauge power consumption. Most of them pilfered electricity by flinging hooks onto the cables. The blobs of light helped Madan to find his way home. His children had gone to sleep after their supper. Kanta was doing the dishes in the light of the clay lamp.

'You have been gone a long while. Where have you been?' Kanta asked Madan when she saw him.

'On my way back from the river I went to Tarsem's home. I have spoken to him about today's affair. Tomorrow he will accompany me to the BDO's office.' Saying this, Madan bent down to enter their hut.

'The children were busy playing throughout the day and got tired. They fell asleep as soon as they had their meal in the evening,' said Kanta. Madan looked at his sleeping children and sat on his cot in silence. He shook off the shoe from one foot and then removed the other shoe with the toes of his bare foot. Sitting on his cot, he removed his loi from his shoulders and placed it at the head of the bed. Then he lifted the quilt from one side and lay down with his sleeping son, Kamal.

Madan was seeing a new ray of light after meeting Tarsem. He was swimming once again in the ocean of his wishes and hopes.

'I have saved some food for you. Shall I bring it here?' Kanta asked Madan, disturbing his daydreaming.

'No, I ate at Tarsem's home,' Madan replied without moving. Gradually, he slid back again into the memories of his childhood.

Bears and Honeybees

Madan was just a child, when his father was in the prime of his youth. Sardari Lal was a strong young man. Those were the days when the 'New Pratap Canal' was being constructed. It was said that the canal would be very useful to poor farmers. Men and women from every village went to work on it with great zeal. Sardari Lal had also worked on the site for quite a long time. 'Every one of us labourers worked with much more enthusiasm there than labourers anywhere else,' Sardari Lal never tired of telling his family.

'During the excavation of the Pratap Canal we used to go to the site early in the morning and offer prayers before the hills of Goddess Vaishno Devi;[1] only then did we commence

1. One of the most popular deities of north India. Her shrine is located in the Trikuta hills and can be seen from the site of the New Pratap Canal. Vaishno Devi is also fondly called 'Mata Rani', meaning Queen Mother.

the day's work,' recalled Sardari Lal. 'Besides, while digging if we came across any big stone or an obstinate stump of a tree, we put all our might against it in the name of the Divine Mother and did not relent till it was uprooted. Many a time when we deposited earth and rubble on the banks, we feared that water from the canal would crash through and wash away everything that stood in its way. After all, can anything endure against fire and water? On such occasions also we remembered Mata Rani to regain our calm. Thus we spent countless weeks—why months and years—together in building the canal as you see it today. We built it with all the zest of our youth,' Sardari Lal's face shone with pride.

'At last, the canal was ready to carry water. When they let water into it for the first time, all the children as well as men and women, young and old, from the surrounding areas were present to witness the spectacle ...' Sardari Lal said. Gradually, the look of joy and pride on his face dimmed. He sighed deeply and paused. One among the eager listeners egged him on, 'What happened after that?'

'After that we got none of the benefits which we were promised at the time of construction,' Sardari Lal replied sadly and fell silent for a moment. From the expression on his face, it was evident that he wanted someone to ask him what benefits he was speaking of. Again a listener asked him the question he was waiting for. Sardari Lal heaved a sigh and began again, 'We used up all our youthful energy to dig and build up this canal. We worked much harder than the worth of the wages we got. All of us who toiled there believed that we would be better off once this work was completed. We didn't know then that we would get nothing beyond the measly wages we were being paid.'

Jamit Raj, who was also listening, asked, 'Chachu, what else did you expect beyond your wages?'

'The construction of this canal carried water to every field in this land. When the rains failed or fell short, the canal water made it possible to irrigate the fields. The water from the canal turned even the barren lands into fertile farms. Today, lush greenery surrounds you wherever you go. Farms are turning out gold. Thanks to the canal that we built, the fields here now yield more than three or four times the quantity of grain that they did earlier. If this is not benefit, then what is?' After another pause, Sardari Lal added, 'But the whole benefit has gone to the people who *owned* land—the zamindars. We had only a plot of four-five *marlas*[2] on which we barely manage to live. We didn't have any land to grow crops.'

Jamit Raj and the other listeners fell to thinking that Sardari Lal was right.

'The government-constructed canal made the rich, land-owners richer. We poor folks got nothing out of it, except that we can bathe in it with our sons during the summer season and draw water from it in places which are far from the wells.' Sardari Lal's deep sigh left the listeners with a heavy feeling that he had been deceived and had lost hope in his old age.

'It's nobody's fault. My own bad luck, that's what it is. I must have done something terrible in a previous life. Now I have to pay for my karma in this life,' Sardari Lal said, blaming himself.

They all agreed with him silently that whatever good or bad was happening to them was the result of the good and bad deeds they had committed in some earlier births.

2. North Indian unit of land—one marla is equal to 25 square yards or 20.903 square metres.

These sentiments changed the topic of their conversation. But Sardari Lal's tale had left an indelible impression on their minds.

About two kilometres from Madan's village was stationed a military brigade. Its gong struck ten. The ten chimes sounded clearly through the night air, breaking the thread of Madan's thoughts. He looked around himself. Kanta had fallen asleep. Lying in bed, when Madan turned towards Kamal the quilt behind him slipped off the mattress. A wave of icy wind pierced him from head to toe. Drawing back a little and gripping the quilt, he covered his back. Then he felt for Kamal's back and after assuring himself that the boy was adequately covered, withdrew his hand.

Madan was floating on the ocean of his thoughts and could not sight land nearby. His father's story had disturbed him too much to permit sleep. To have been fobbed off with paltry wages for all that sweat and labour which had transformed the once barren land into lush fields!

'We have been unlucky all along. If only our elders also had been tillers, we too would have got land to farm,' Madan thought sadly.

He went back to the times when he was very young and could not go alone to town. Those days the village patwari had enlisted in his revenue records the names of those of Zaildar Dayaram's workmen who were engaged in reaping and sowing on his farms for several years. On the basis of the patwari's records, the government had in the year 1971 declared these peasants masters of the lands they had been tilling. Now the zamindars did not have any right whatsoever on the lands they had once owned.

When Salt Loses its Taste

It was the talk of the day. Chief Minister, Sheikh Mohammed Abdullah was going to declare that the peasants who laboured in the fields of the landowners would be accorded ownership of the lands they tilled.

Jangi was the same age as Madan's father, Sardari Lal, and he had been the best man at Sardari Lal's wedding. It was he who had untied the bridegroom's *gana*[1] from Sardari Lal's wrist. Jangi lived in the same village and had come to their home. Both Jangi and Sardari Lal sat talking excitedly to each other. Madan grew curious and leaving his game, entered the hut and sat close to his elders to hear what they were saying.

---

1. Ritual bands tied round the wrists of the bride and groom to ward off the evil eye. At the end of the wedding ceremonies, the bands are unfastened by the friend/*saheli* (woman-friend) of the groom and the bride who are specially chosen for the occasion.

'Our own *Jenab* Sheikh Mohammed Abdullah sahib is coming here in person this Monday. His party men are out in every lane and by-lane to announce his visit on vehicle-mounted loudspeakers. They say Sheikh Sahib would be addressing a large gathering and will personally distribute land ownership deeds to the peasants,' said Jangi.

The zamindars were not pleased since their vast closely-held inheritance was about to slip through their hands. Men whom they had been ordering about were now to become masters of *their* land in their own right. The lands they had been getting tilled by the peasants would no longer be under their sway.

The farmhands, though, were excited because the promise of owning land had lain beyond their fondest dreams. They had been like slaves. Now, in one stroke, they would be owners of lands they had laboured on. But they celebrated the glad tidings quietly in their homes among their own kith and kin.

'I have heard something else,' Jangi said to Sardari Lal. 'Some zamindars go about bragging that Jenab Sheikh Mohammed Abdullah might well give away the land deeds to the landless, but *they* would see how the newly turned landlords would take possession of those lands.' His narrow wrinkled face reflected anxiety.

Madan heard his elders, but could understand nothing. It was all quite beyond him.

Sardari Lal and Jangi talked for a long time. Then Jangi left for his home.

On Monday, a large number of people set out in the direction of the town. There was no tarred road in the hamlet and the *kucha* lanes did not permit any buses or lorries to ply.

Jangi came again to Sardari Lal's home and they made plans to attend Chief Minister Sheikh Abdullah's public meeting.

When Madan heard of their intention, he persisted, 'I also want to go. I too want to see Sheikh Abdullah.'

'Sardari Lal, let's take Maddi along with us,' said Jangi. 'He is a little boy after all; let's take him around the town.'

Sardari Lal agreed with Jangi that Madan might accompany them. Leaving the village, they proceeded towards the city along with countless others.

A huge crowd had gathered in the school ground where the public meeting was to be held. The place had no boundary wall. Spilling out of the ground, they sat on the canal bank and even beyond, till the roadside.

When Sheikh Sahib's car arrived in a cloud of dust, there was a surge of excitement in the gathering. People raised slogans as the leader alighted from his vehicle and approached the stage. Someone shouted over the microphone, 'Sheikh Sahib!'

'Zindabad!' the public responded.

'The Lion of Kashmir!'

'Long live the Lion of Kashmir!'

'He's here, brother, he's here!'

'The Lion of Kashmir is here!'

People raised slogans repeatedly. Sardari Lal, Jangi, and Madan stood at a distance from the stage. Madan could not make out who Sheikh Abdullah was. For a while, the crowd seemed to be getting out of hand but gradually it grew peaceful. Loud speakers blared out endlessly: 'Please be seated!'

People close to the stage began to sit down. Those standing behind them followed suit. Sardari Lal lifted Madan on to his shoulder and said, 'The tallest man you see on the stage, the one who with a fur cap—that one is our own Sheikh Abdullah.'

'Which one?' Madan asked again.

'The one in a long coat, my son. The tallest man out there.'

Clad in a black *achkan*[2] with a *Karakuli* cap,[3] Chief Minister Sheikh Abdullah made a distinguished presence on the stage. Other men standing on the stage barely reached his shoulders. With a broad smile on his face, he waved in warm response to the greetings of the audience.

Madan couldn't recall much of that meeting except that Jangi too had gone up to the stage and stood by Sheikh Sahib's side.

Memories of things that had happened the following day and were discussed on every occasion later were etched on Madan's mind. Barbers, carpenters, blacksmiths, and odd-job men—jheewars—had not received the land deeds as they were not directly engaged in the tilling of land and harvesting of crops, neither did they figure in the revenue records. Workmen who did not find a place in the revenue records were denied land. Sardari Lal used to vent his anger quite often at home, 'What if we did not hold a sickle in our hands, we too have been working in the fields! Who served water to those who plied sickles and ploughs in the fields? We did. At weddings and other functions we performed odd jobs. What kind of a government policy is this that one person gets land and another in the same village gets nothing?'

The gong at the military brigade grounds struck, ruffling Madan's thoughts once again. It was eleven o'clock at night— rather late for him to be awake. The whole village was in deep slumber. He could hear dogs howling at a distance. Riding the train of his thoughts, he did not know when sleep overtook him.

---

2. A knee-length, close fitting coat worn by men.
3. Made of the skin of an unborn Karakul lamb.

Madan got up at his accustomed time early in the morning, even though he had slept quite late the previous night. In the greyness of the predawn hours, he began his routine of going out to fish in the river in the freezing cold.

Madan returned home when it was bright daylight. Sipping tea, he sat waiting for Tarsem. The village boys had left for their school one by one. Not having a watch, he could only guess it was ten o'clock. He got tired of waiting for Tarsem. Picking up the parcel of fish and wrapping a light blanket around himself, he set out for Tarsem's house.

Kanta, Madan's wife, sat in her tuala, arching her neck keenly to watch him going his way till he disappeared from her sight. Once again, she sought hope in her despair.

Tarsem's house had neither boundary wall, nor any entry gate. Madan walked straight into the compound. Seated on a cot spread out in the sun, Tarsem was having his breakfast. He invited Madan also to sit with him. 'Please make yourself comfortable here itself,' he told Madan.

Madan saw Tarsem's mother who was also sunning herself nearby, 'Chachi, perain pauna,' he said to her and proceeded to sit on the cot close to Tarsem.

'Toshi, bring one more platter for brother Madan,' Tarsem called to his younger sister, Santosh, who was seated with his mother.

Madan was hungry but he said to them, 'No, Toshi, no. Don't bring anything for me. I just had my breakfast before coming here.'

Tarsem knew well that in Madan's home, cooking started only when he had sold his fish and brought home rations for the day. He understood that Madan was fighting shy of eating at his place. He said to him, 'Eat a little more with me.' 'Bring him some breakfast,' he said, turning to Santosh.

Seated on the cot, Madan ate three or four *parathas*[4] and then took a cup of tea. The vegetable-oil parathas were a treat for him. He rubbed off the traces of oil on both his hands and then smeared his head as well with the remnants by coursing his oily hands through his hair.

Tarsem finished his breakfast and went inside the house to change. He came out combing his hair.

After a short while, they set out for the city. The sun was at its highest point in the sky over them and the temperature had risen.

They reached the city talking to each other. The one question that had engaged Madan's mind during the whole journey was whether the much talked-about government plan would fetch the cheque for building a pukka house for himself.

On reaching the town, Madan left Tarsem in the bazaar for ten to fifteen minutes and proceeded towards Thorhu's eatery.

Thorhu was busy with his pots simmering on his ovens. It was time for him to prepare lunch. Panju, his servant, sliced onions into a large tray inside the shop, his eyes watering from the onion fumes. He turned his head painfully from side to side and pressed his eyes and then blinked hard. The smoky ovens and onion slicing had made his eyes red.

Madan went straight into the dhaba and emptied his bundle of fish. Thorhu came inside once. Glancing at the fish, he went back to the door and began to stir the boiling dal.

Madan himself put all his fish into a big empty pot and stood by Thorhu's side, waiting to be paid.

Thorhu turned to look at Madan. Slipping his hand into pocket of his kurta, he took out two fifty-rupee notes and

4. Fried unleavened bread.

handed them to Madan. Madan put the money into his pocket and walked back to Tarsem.

By this time the bazaar was buzzing with activity. When he arrived there, Madan found that Tarsem had been waiting for him.

It was about eleven o'clock when both Madan and Tarsem reached the BDO's office which was in the bazaar. At this time of the day, the office appeared to be nearly empty.

The minister had visited the place only the day before. How then would any employee reach the office that early! Tarsem and Madan sat waiting for the BDO with hardly four clerks and peons present in the office. Some five or six people from Madan's village were standing outside the BDO's office. Madan knew Chimmo as they had both worked for daily wages. From the conversation of the other men there it appeared that they too were daily-wage earners.

The BDO arrived at about one o'clock in the afternoon. With his arrival, employees who had been dawdling in the bazaar also entered the office and it was now abuzz with activity.

Bidding namaste to the BDO, Tarsem entered his room. Madan too offered his respects with folded hands.

'How are you?' the BDO asked Madan, recognizing him.

Madan responded to the polite inquiry and stood deferentially before the official. Tarsem took a seat. On the BDO's invitation, Madan sat down near Tarsem.

The BDO was seated on a revolving chair behind a huge table. He rang the bell placed before him and a peon came running in response.

'Call Babu Mansa Ram.'

'Yes sir. I'll fetch him this moment,' said the peon while leaving the room.

After a few moments, a bespectacled and paunchy middle-aged man entered the room.

'Mansa Ram,' said the BDO, 'this man is not on the list of persons who received cheques for pukka houses yesterday. Please look into the file and tell me why he is not there.'

'In a moment, sir,' replied the man. Passing Madan on his way out, he asked him, 'Tell me your name please.'

'My name is Madan Lalji.'

'Your father's name and the village you live?'

On receiving the details, Babu Mansa Ram left the room and returned in ten to fifteen minutes. Standing before BDO's table, he waited for his turn to speak, as the BDO was talking to someone else. After finishing his conversation, the BDO gave him a questioning look.

'Sir, he does not have a BPL number,' Babu Mansa Ram said to his superior, explaining why Madan had not received the cheque.

'Do you have a BPL ration card?' the BDO asked Madan.

'No, I don't, *Jenab*,' Madan said, shaking his head. He was still not clear what it all meant and whether he would receive the cheque.

'He has not been allotted a BPL number. A villager who does not have a BPL number is not entitled to receive financial help for constructing a pukka house,' the BDO disposed of the matter summarily and looked at Madan and Tarsem as if he had achieved something.

It was turning out exactly as Madan had feared. His mouth went dry and his mind turned blank.

Tarsem took up the issue on Madan's behalf. He told the BDO that Madan was indeed very poor. He lived in an old hut and was in utter penury. If he still could not get a BPL certificate, asked Tarsem, was there any ground or procedure to make him eligible for the scheme?

'It's immaterial whether one is really poor, or not. If a person doesn't have a BPL certificate, he doesn't get a cheque for constructing a concrete house. That's it.' The BDO reiterated his decision in a matter-of-fact manner.

In the conversation that lasted ten to fifteen minutes, Tarsem came to understand that there was no use dragging the matter any further with the official. He felt they should leave the office.

Stepping out of the room, Tarsem said to the BDO, 'Thank you, very much!' The BDO looked away and replied, 'You are welcome.'

Tarsem came out of the BDO's office. Madan also got up. Bidding namaste to the BDO with folded hands, he also went out of the room. He joined Tarsem in a few long strides and asked him, 'Tell me, Tarsem, what is this BPL number?'

'BPL or the Below Poverty Line number identifies a family that is poorer than the country's poor. This number entitles a family to a special ration card.'

Deep in their talk, Madan and Tarsem had reached the bazaar. Tarsem was hungry. Finding Rampal Khajuria's tea stall in front of them, Tarsem invited Madan for a cup of tea so that they could finish talking.

Madan was also hungry, as he had had parathas hours ago in the morning. He nodded in agreement as they arrived at Khajuria's shop.

Entering the tea stall, they sat to the right of the room against the wall on two chairs opposite each other. Between them was a grimy teapoy on which stood a used teacup.

The tea counter, a kerosene stove on it, was on the left side. A soot-blackened aluminium kettle, filled with water, sat on the stove from dawn to dusk. Behind the counter stood Rampal Khajuria making tea and on the wall on his right were fixed wooden planks which served as shelves for glass jars full of snacks such as *matthis* and *kachoris*. An entire shelf held matchboxes and cigarette packets. The lowest shelf was full of unsold crates of soda water bottles from the last summer. Flies generally didn't bother one in winter, but this particular shop was thick with flies because of splashes of sugary tea.

Finding two customers in his stall, Rampal Khajuria withdrew a dirty rag from under the counter and approached their table. Standing close to them, he bent over to pick up the used cup with one hand and cleaned the tabletop with the other.

'Two cups of tea and two matthis,' Tarsem placed their order.

Rampal Khajuria returned to his counter with the used cups and began to make tea.

Tarsem picked up the thread of his conversation. 'I was saying that the Government of India has taken a count of people who live below the poverty line. Every such family has been issued a number. Along with this number is issued a ration card. These ration cards fetch rations at a low cost, since the government itself subsidizes rations meant for the BPL persons. An ordinary ration card fetches a family its ration every month; in the same manner, the BPL families are also entitled to monthly rations against their special cards.'

Madan mentally calculated that he could not afford to buy a week's rations for his family in a single purchase. The BPL rations might be dirt cheap, but how would he manage enough money to buy rations for a full month?

Perhaps that was the reason that even though some people in the village had got their ration cards made, Madan had neither gone for his BPL ration card, nor had he spoken to

anyone about its significance. Never before had he heard
about the government's census of the families which were
extremely poor and the plans that had been made on the
basis of that census for improving their lot. Madan did not
know, nor had he bothered to know, when and how the census was conducted. He had heard somewhere that one could
get low-cost rations against a BPL card. Beyond that he knew
nothing.

That day, Madan realized that his greatest dream of having
a pukka house would remain unfulfilled because his name
did not appear in the BPL list.

'Is it possible at this stage to have a BPL ration card issued
in my name?' Madan asked Tarsem, seeking a way out of his
perplexity.

Barely a few years ago Tarsem's own family had also been
living below the poverty line. Their economic condition
had improved only when he had found a job. Tarsem could
understand the problems of the very poor.

Tarsem realized from Madan's question that the man
was desperate to secure a cheque under the government's
scheme for pukka houses. He did not take Madan's probing
merely as a question, but shared acutely the very emotions
and the helplessness of his kin that had brought forth such
a query. He took care not to hurt Madan's feelings while
answering him.

Rampal Khajuria approached carrying cups of tea in both
hands. He put down the cups on the teapoy, one before
Tarsem and the other before Madan. The slight disturbance
caused the flies to buzz lazily in the same space for a moment,
only to settle down again on the small table. Rampal Khajuria
went back to his counter to bring back a plate of two matthis
which too he placed before them.

Inviting Madan to drink his tea, Tarsem also picked up the teacup placed before him and took a sip of the scalding brew.

Madan looked at Tarsem without blinking in the hope of an answer—an answer that could provide a ray of hope for him.

Tarsem replaced the teacup on the table. Putting an end to Madan's wait, he said, 'They don't make BPL ration cards every day. About four years ago, a census was carried out on the government's orders. On the basis of the data collected, a list was made of the families living below the poverty line in the whole country. The listing was done by government officials themselves. Some of them had come to our village as well when they took down the names of the needy families.'

Madan searched his memory; he was surprised at Tarsem's revelation. He had been totally unaware of the goings on in his own village.

Thinking harder, Madan said, 'I never saw anyone coming to the village to register our names. If someone did come, how could he have missed me for being anything other than a poor man? I own neither land nor have I an inheritance and I definitely do not have a government job. I have four small children but no pukka house for them. We live in a thatched hut. Every day, I go out to earn a wage by the sweat of my brow. Only then a fire burns in my hearth and only then do we have food in our bellies. Biroomal and those who have received cheques to build pukka houses are all better off than I am. The village priest Ram Krishan is by no means poor. He already has a pukka house. All the offerings at the temple go to him.'

Madan's outpouring touched Tarsem. He seemed to be at a loss for words.

When Tarsem gestured to Madan reminding him about his tea, he raised his cup and took a sip. Tarsem moved the matthi plate towards him and Madan accepted one as well. Taking a deep bite, he munched on it with another sip of tea. Madan was keen on grasping Tarsem's reply.

Tarsem also wished that Madan could receive a cheque for a pukka house. But he did not have a straight answer to Madan's question. Unlettered though he was, Madan would have to himself struggle to collect all those details which had come to Tarsem readily because of his education. Tarsem had got a government job after finishing his university education and was well versed with the intricacies of the official maze as well as society's cast-iron structure. .

To this day our society has not turned truly democratic, thought Tarsem. We take decisions on the basis of caste and religion and these national and social flaws in our public conduct influence the government decisions as well. Politics too is in a state of decline. Government runs schemes to benefit all the citizens in equal measure, but the political parties, particularly the ones in power, twist and turn the schemes in such a manner as to garner all benefits for their own workers and supporters. And finally, this sort of administrative discrimination becomes the undoing of the grandest, finest, and biggest schemes. But Madan was innocent of all these pitfalls of public good.

At last, Tarsem began to answer Madan. 'When the census officials came to our village, they all went straight to the house of Sarpanch Gulchain Singh, the village headman, and under his supervision filled up those forms for the villagers below poverty line. Biroomal is BPL and works in the Sarpanch's fields. He does nothing without first consulting Gulchain Singh, so much so that when the Parliamentary elections were held last year, Biroomal cast his vote at Gulchain Singh's bidding.'

Tarsem paused for a while after making this disclosure. He took a bite of the matthi and began to munch on it with another sip of tea.

Madan watched Tarsem's face unblinkingly. He waited keenly for Tarsem to continue.

'Suman Verma is Kailash Nath Verma's wife. She is educated and already owns a house. But as you know, she lost her husband just a few years after her marriage. No one can have any objection to a widow getting her cheque.' Tarsem added.

'How has Ram Krishan's name appeared in the list of BPL families?' Madan asked again.

Tarsem reminded Madan of the uneaten matthi he was holding. He himself bit into his matthi and began to chew it. Taking another sip of tea, he said, 'Purohit Ram Krishan is priest to the whole village. At every harvest, the sarpanch and other members of the panchayat, the zaildar[5] and all the peasants set apart a share for him before they take the grain to their houses. The priest keeps some grain for his personal use and sells the rest to the traders. Be it a *punya, kadashi, massya*[6] or any other festival, villagers make offerings to the temple, all of which go eventually to Ram Krishan. Whatever is special here goes first to the purohit and then only elsewhere. How then could Purohit Ram Krishna be denied something which the government offers to the villagers? His name must appear before any other beneficiary.'

---

5. An important revenue functionary from the days of the British raj.
6. Important days in the Hindu calendar: the full moon day, the eleventh day, and the no-moon day, respectively.

They had finished their tea during this long conversation and placed their empty cups on the saucers on the teapoy. Neither of them wanted to linger. Moving out of the narrow space between the teapoy and the chairs, they walked to the door. Tarsem stood close to Rampal Khajuria and extracting a currency note from his trouser pocket, gave it to Khajuria. Madan stood behind Tarsem.

Rampal Khajuria slipped the currency note into his cashbox. After making a calculation, he gave the balance to Tarsem.

Tarsem pocketed the change and came out of the shop. Madan followed him. They proceeded towards Desu Shah's shop.

'The names of Bhimu and Baldev did not figure in the list of below poverty line persons because they had cast their votes in favour of a candidate of their own choice, in spite of Gulchain Singh telling them to vote for his candidate,' Tarsem said in an effort to explain to Madan the background of the case.

Tarsem's statement only honed Madan's curiosity. Madan had himself witnessed the goings-on, but it was the first time he was grasping their consequence. The two men were now climbing the raised platform of Desu Shah's shop. They ceased all talk on the subject upon entering the shop.

As usual, Madan bowed his head and said namaste to the shopkeeper. Tarsem also bade namaste to the Shah.

'Namaste, Masterji, how do you do? Where are you serving these days? It seems you are on leave,' said the Shah, when he saw Tarsem in his shop.

Tarsem responded courteously to the shopkeeper's polite inquiries and then sat on a bench in front of him.

Madan bought wheat flour and other things and paid in cash. After the transaction, they got up to leave.

'Masterji, please sit down for a while. I'll get you a cup of tea,' Desu Shah said while Madan and Tarsem walked out of his shop.

Tarsem knew that whenever any customer came to his shop after a long time, Desu Shah was wont to ask him for tea, irrespective of how long the customer sat with him. It was a different matter that he had never actually seen the shopkeeper offering tea to anyone.

Tarsem walked down the two low steps of Desu Shah's shop to the bazaar. Madan followed him.

It was already past noon. With the sun beginning to descend on its westward journey, it was less cold at this point of time than the rest of the day.

Madan had nothing more to do in the bazaar, nor did Tarsem. They started to walk back to their village. After a few steps, they walked side by side.

Glancing to the left, Tarsem caught a glimpse of Madan's face walking by him. Madan was also looking at Tarsem. His serious expression reflected a single question, 'What's going to happen now?'

Before a word could escape Madan's lips, Tarsem went on, 'I was saying that Bhimu and Baldev did not cast their votes at Gulchain Singh's bidding and Gulchain in turn suppressed their names appear from the list of BPL families.'

On hearing about the sarpanch and other people of the village, the one question that arose repeatedly in Madan's mind was why these people attached so much importance to being listed 'below poverty line' families. What did men like the sarpanch, Bhima, the purohit, and Baldev have to do with that list?

As soon as Tarsem finished his account, Madan popped his question, 'You said it is the government people who make the list of families living below the poverty line. They do not belong to any political party. Then should they not treat everyone equally? Treat all of us without any bias?' Voicing his innermost concerns, Madan became emotional.

Tarsem looked again at Madan and found that rather than facing him to receive an answer, Madan was pensively looking straight ahead at a patch of grass.

Madan's face reflected the turbulence of his mind and Tarsem understood that he had lost interest in the discussion. Tarsem walked silently along with him towards the village.

Madan was wordless, but a din of questions was confounding his mind, 'How could the officer who had come to prepare the BPL list be so casual? If only that man had visited our lane, he wouldn't have missed my home. He would have seen my thatched hut. He would have seen how my little children live in that miserable hut. Would he have, after seeing all that, still denied me the BPL status?'

Madan pondered, 'Does that government officer know that his omission of one name in the list of families below poverty line has deprived as many as six souls of the barest necessities of life? Would he be able to make up for my loss today if he realized the gravity of his omission?'

Reading Madan's face, Tarsem sensed the turmoil he was undergoing. Tarsem himself was no stranger to the experience. Yet for all his empathy with Mohan, he could neither offer him any relief nor explain to him all the complexities involved at once.

On his part, Madan after denigrating those government officials wondered whether *all* government officers were as irresponsible and callous. He himself sent his children to school and wanted them to become important officers after finishing their studies.

Madan was so deep in thought that he did not realize they had reached the village square, or that Tarsem had parted from him to go the path leading to his own home.

'No! No!' he said aloud to no one in particular and was surprised at his own voice.

Madan was answering his own fear: his children, when they finished their studies and became officers in the government, would they also behave like the officers who had prepared the list of families living below the poverty line in their village?

A Bonsai No More

The wings of time ... Madan had begun to believe that he would get no benefit at all, ever, from any of the government schemes. He ascribed it to his luck and as a payback for the bad deeds of a previous birth. God had willed that he should live in want and misery.

Reconciled though he was to his fate, he nursed a desire that his children should receive a good education, get government jobs, and become officers. He had personally seen other people getting important jobs and felt that one day this dream of his might come true.

Before him was Tarsem's example. If only he, Madan, had also been educated like his cousin, Madan thought, his life would have been comfortable. Education would have made him a man of means and he would not have been down and out as he was. Fully alive to the power of formal learning,

Madan wanted his children to get an education and come out of the morass of poverty by dint of hard work.

About five months had passed since that bleak day when Madan had failed to receive the cheque for a pukka house. It was evening time and he was seated in a relaxed mood with his wife in their tuala. Their children were playing outside with other children of the neighbourhood, except the youngest, Louku, who was with them in the tuala. Kanta was boiling rice. With the corner of her head-cloth she set aside the lid of the pot and stirred the boiling rice. Then she put away the ladle in the hole beside the mud stove and turned towards her husband purposefully.

'I have been thinking for the past few days,' Kanta began, 'that what you earn as a daily wager or by selling fish is not enough to meet our expenses even for a day. The children are growing up. They eat as much as adults. Won't it be good if we grew paddy this time on two-four *kanals*[1] on one-fourth share basis?' She pushed a piece of wood into the fire.

Madan looked at her intently.

'We could get two-three sacks of paddy through share-cropping. Louku is old enough now. I won't have any problem with him,' Kanta added, looking at Louku.

'You are right. If our share is that much paddy, we would be saving the cost of a year's supply of rice,' Madan commented on her suggestion and then went on to express his own concern, 'But it won't be that easy, Kanta. If both of us get busy planting, where are we going to find money to meet our daily expenses?'

It was Madan himself who found a way out. He spoke to Jamit Raj who too was engaged in share-cropping. The families

1. A kanal is 5,400 square feet or one-eighth of an acre.

of Madan and Jamit Raj jointly took some land and planted paddy. Kamal and Kamlesh also helped out and after the harvest, Madan's family got about one and half sacks of paddy as their share. Kanta's had been a major contribution towards the venture.

In this manner the family got its own stock of rice for more than half a year. The money they saved went to other things they needed.

They sowed paddy the following year as well. Again Kamal and Kamlesh helped in the field with their little, delicate hands. After the harvest they got two sacks of paddy which was slightly more than their share of the previous year.

Years went by in this manner. Madan's children were growing up. They worked with their parents in the paddy fields. Besides, Madan brought home some additional money as a daily wager and supplemented his income by selling fish that he caught in the river.

The children started going to school. It was Madan's desire to send all his children to school and it fell to Tarsem to fulfil his desire. He paid their fees, and continued to support the children when they went on to the next and the next higher classes. Madan got his children second-hand books at half the price from the village children who had passed on to the next class.

Madan's children—Kamal, Kamlesh, Usha, and Louku—did well at the government school. Kamal always stood among the first five in the exams.

* * *

Kamal was now in the eighth class. This exam was common to all the schools in the zone and he had to go to the town to write the exam along with other children from his village.

On the day of the results, Kamal again set out in his worn clothes. Although he had done well in his class throughout the year, he was not too sure how well he would fare in a zonal exam. Even the teachers who had handed out the question papers were from other schools. Still, he had begun to like the big school and decided to seek admission there once he passed the eighth grade.

The sky was overcast with clouds and the sun was hidden. When Kamal reached the big school in town, it was already packed with children who had come from all over the zone to learn their results. A school master stood on the stage which was normally used for the morning assembly. The clouds grew denser in the sky and the weather became pleasant. The students sat on the ground in front of the stage and waited. The school master announced that he would first read out the names of the students who had stood first, second, and third in the exam.

'Rajendra Kumar has scored the highest marks and stands first,' the teacher proclaimed and added, 'Rajendra Kumar, please stand up and come to the stage.'

Rajendra Kumar, son of a teacher of a school in the town, got up and made his way to the stage through the throng of students. The teacher on the stage and the students sitting in their rows on the ground greeted Rajendra Kumar with warm applause. Rajendra stood on the stage. He had topped his class from the day he entered school.

'Prakash Chand stands the second! Prakash Chand, come to the stage,' said the school master.

Prakash Chand was the son of Bansi Lal, a compounder employed with the local hospital. People generally called him 'Doctor Bansi'. Prakash too was a student of a town school. He also stood up and made his way to the stage. There was loud clapping again. As he had done to Rajendra Kumar, the teacher patted Prakash Chand on the back.

'The third place goes to Kamal Dev. Kamal Dev, step up to the stage!' Minutes went by but no one stood up. The school master repeated the boy's name and the name of the school to which he belonged.

Kamal could not believe that the name being called from the stage was his own and no one else's. At that moment, a teacher from his own school scanned the crowd and finding him out called, 'Kamal Dev, get up, please!'

The teacher on the stage and the mass of students on the ground were waiting to see who that Kamal Dev was. Was he there or not?

Hearing the voice of Kamal's school teacher, the boys turned their eyes towards the direction where Kamal was seated.

It still did not fully register with Kamal that among all the candidates of the zone who had appeared for the eighth-class exam, he had attained the third rank. Drawing courage from his teacher's call, he walked up to the stage.

Again there was loud clapping and all the children looked towards the stage. The teacher on the stage patted Kamal on the back.

When at last Kamal was certain of his astonishing success, his happiness knew no bounds. His feet planted firmly on earth, he began to fly in the air.

The teacher went on calling out the names of each one of the students of the eighth class and read out their results. He also told them the date for admission to the ninth class. All the teachers then proceeded to the headmaster's room while the students went back happily to their homes.

The town boys began to discuss Kamal Dev's achievement. Teachers too were amazed at how the son of a man who sold fish and worked for daily wages could outrank a host of students from the zone.

Happiness exploded in Kamal's heart. He wanted to share his joy with someone. But there was no friend or a relative around him—all his kin were away. Perhaps his score in the exam was not that important for his family, he thought, as he tried to take his mind away from the little affair.

In the morning when he had come to the school for his result, Kamal had planned to take a round of the bazaar before going home. He took a hurried round of the bazaar and then turned homewards. The clouds were now getting thicker and it started to rain presently. Half way home, he was drenched in the downpour.

The potholes on the unpaved road were filled with muddy water, making it difficult for anyone to walk on. But the path leading to the house of the village headman was fun to traverse, paved as it was with cement tiles. Rainwater flowed from the pavement to the gutter, washing the pavement clean as if someone had washed and scrubbed it.

But when he left the pavement to take the path home, his feet stuck in the mud and slush. The blending of rainwater, mud, and dung of the passing cattle was thick like the gummy mix used by the villagers to plaster their mud houses. Taking each step precariously with his pair of old nylon slippers, Kamal approached his house. In comparison to the lane outside, his compound was somewhat better as the cattle did not seem to have trudged over the wet clay there.

But there was not the slightest difference between the compound and the inside of the hut. The worn out thatch leaked like a sieve. Water poured out of every hole. Tumblers, pots, and other utensils had been kept on the floor with the hope that water would fall only into them and leave the floor dry. But it had rained so heavily and for so long that such devices proved useless. The mud floor was covered with a thick layer of water. At some places, the sharp cataract had dug holes into the mud-plastered floor. The bedding had been gathered in a relatively dry corner. But even there small leakages had left it partially wet.

Traversing the compound, Kamal bent down slightly and entered into the hut. The first thing he noticed inside was that water was dripping over his schoolbag. Hurriedly, he took down his khaki satchel from a *giddi*.[2] Opening it, he found that the books and the notebooks had become soggy. He had carefully preserved these books all through the year hoping to make some money by selling them at half the price when he passed the exam. Regretfully, Kamal opened a notebook and found that the blue ink of his notes had clouded its pages.

Kamal dropped his schoolbag and came out hurriedly. From behind the hearth he brought three-four pieces of wood and laid them under the cot which had the bedding on it. He spread the soaked books over the wood pieces to let them dry up. Then he removed his wet clothes and changed into the worn-out school uniform which hung from a clothes line, spreading out his wet clothes to dry on the firewood stored behind the hearth.

* * *

The sun was about to set. Madan, who had gone to work with Manga Mistri, had still not returned home. Kamal's mother Kanta, his two younger sisters, and a younger brother were home. Their clothes were dripping with water spewing from the roof and leaking from numerous holes in the hut.

2. Y-shaped wooden poles which support the ridge of the sloping roof of a hut.

It was time to cook the evening meal, but the firewood stored behind the hearth was dripping wet. Kanta had rescued some wood during the rainfall and brought it inside, but those pieces were also damp.

The rainfall had stopped at last after doing its job. Wisps of clouds floated about in the sky. As they were dispersing gradually, patches of blue could be seen in the grey skies.

Kanta came out of the hut and went to the tuala. Sitting down, she removed two pieces of sacking placed over the mud stove. She also put aside a worn-out basket to find that the mud stove was completely dry, though the rest of the earth around it was wet.

Kanta got up and brought the logs she had kept inside the hut. She also brought some wet logs from behind the hearth and got busy kindling a fire.

When the rain stopped, Louku and Usha heard the voices of other children and went out to play with them.

Kamal and Kamlesh stayed back to help their mother, struggling hard to ignite wet fuel.

The sun had set and darkness was spreading.

'*Bhapa*[3] has come! Bhapa has come!' cried out Louku who was playing in the compound. Usha also was playing with him. Kamal and Kamlesh raised their heads and looked out of the hearth.

'Look, he solves our problem!' Kanta exclaimed. She was particularly happy to see her husband at that moment.

That day Madan had been at a construction site, where work on doors and windows was going on. At the day's end,

---

3. A respectful term for an older brother. Here, the children use it for their father, in keeping with the custom prevalent in the rural areas of the region.

Madan had made himself a small bundle of the discarded wood chips and pieces and brought it home. It was dry pinewood with which Kanta could light a fire with ease.

Louku and Usha came to the tuala along with their father. Madan put aside the day's rations and the bundle of tinder on the ground and sat down.

The pinewood helped start a fire in the stove and in the radiating heat the wet logs also began to dry.

In Madan's home food was cooked twice a day, morning and evening. The family was used to having their evening meal rather early. But that day it had taken too long to build up a fire strong enough for cooking. Kanta had just begun. Seeing that some sort of order had been restored in her house, she wanted to share with her husband something which was uppermost in her mind.

'Now our Kamal would start going to the town's school. We will have to buy him books and the uniform,' she said to Madan who was sitting close to the stove.

Madan knew that the result of Kamal's eighth class was due. Kamal's school teachers in the village always had a word of praise for the boy. Madan was confident that Kamal would pass. That was the reason he had not asked about the boy's result. Now that his wife brought the matter out in the open, his first reaction was to worry how he would meet the boy's school requirements.

There was a faint trace of anxiety on Kanta's face too. But an assurance also lurked in some corner of her mind. As before, she hoped, Tarsem would visit them and not only pay Kamal's admission fees, but also buy him books and the uniform.

'I'll get my two days' wages and buy Kamal's books myself,' Madan said with pride. Kanta too was proud that they would be able to meet Kamal's expenses.

Keeping up with the mood of the moment, Kamal narrated the day's events to his parents and the siblings. He had got the third position among the students of the eighth class who had passed the exam. The school master of the town's big school had called him to the stage and patted his back. All the other children there had given him a thunderous applause. There were just two other boys who had been called to the stage.

Kamal had wanted to share the happy news with everyone at home. But wading through all those annoying problems since the afternoon, he had found his achievement was of little significance. In fact, he had come to think it was not such a big success after all. It would not provide a roof over their open hearth, or get him a school uniform. How could his happiness have lasted in such conditions? Lighting a fire and cooking meal at that time was a success much bigger than passing an exam with distinction.

Kamlesh got up from where she had been sitting in the tuala and went inside the hut to sit on a cot. She was feeling sleepy. Louku and Usha were already asleep there.

'Kamlesh, my little one, don't fall asleep,' Madan went after her and tried to keep her awake, 'your meal is ready.'

Kamlesh, stretched on the bed, made no response. She knew it would take at the very least half an hour more for the meal to be ready.

Kamal was not much older, but the conditions at home and its responsibilities had made him wise before his time. He was waiting silently for the food to be cooked, planning all the while how he would go to the big school far away in the town.

The weather had cleared now. There were hardly any traces of clouds in the sky.

The supper was ready. Kamal was served first.

'Kamlesh! Usha! Louku! Get up. Food is ready. Come and eat.' Kanta called her children while ladling out food on their plates.

Kamal was famished by now. It had been a long wait. He began to eat as soon he was served.

When none of the children inside the hut came out in spite of Kanta's repeated calls, Madan himself got up and went inside the hut to wake them up.

'Kamlesh, my dear, get up. Mother has prepared sweet rice with jaggery. Eat and then you may go to sleep again. Don't sleep on an empty stomach.' Madan tugged at Kamlesh's arm trying to make her sit up.

But at that time children loved their sleep more than sweet rice. Kamlesh lay down again as soon Madan let go her arm.

Madan tried to wake up Usha also in this manner, but she too dropped off to sleep.

Then Madan picked up his youngest child Louku in both his arms and bringing him into the tuala, placed him in Kanta's lap. With some effort Kanta was able to put some rice into the sleepy child's mouth.

Then Madan also fed Kamlesh and Usha in the same manner while they were asleep.

Madan was glad they could cook in spite of the heavy rain. Half asleep though they were, the children did have some food. It was not like the day a dust storm had blown throughout the night, and made it impossible to cook. Kanta and Madan too had their meal.

Having eaten, Kanta spread a dry piece of cloth over the children's cot and was left with nothing for her own bed.

* * *

On the appointed day, Kamal took money from his father and secured admission in the town school. The children admitted to the school were called for classes the following day.

Tarsem had not come home on leave even once after Kamal's success in the eighth class exam, which meant that Kamal could not get books for the ninth class.

On the second day of his admission, Kamal went to the school. The ninth class had three sections, 'A', 'B', and 'C'. Kamal was enrolled as number one in Section 'C'.

On the very first day when the students sat at their desks in the allotted classrooms, the class teacher asked by way of getting acquainted with them, which schools they had attended earlier. He had heard that Kamal was the son of a very poor fisherman, and highly intelligent. The boy had ranked third in the last exam among the candidates of the entire zone. The boys who were first and second in the exam had received private tuitions for eight to ten months during the year. But this boy had secured the third position entirely on his own in the midst of many struggles.

After the introduction, Master Banarsi Dass asked him, 'Kamal, have you purchased books for the ninth class?'

It was the first day at school and his first meeting with the teacher. The question made Kamal self-conscious. He ought to have bought the books. Standing by his desk, Kamal was pondering whether he should admit the truth.

'No, sir,' he replied after a pause. Having found the courage to speak the truth, Kamal waited for the teacher's orders.

'Good. Son, this time I will give you the books for the ninth class as a reward for attaining the third position in the zone,' declared Banarsi Dass happily.

Kamal not only heaved a sigh of relief but also felt a surge of happiness at the prospect of getting a set of books free of charge.

Detailing a peon to the bazaar, Banarsi Dass bought an entire set of books and notebooks that had been prescribed for the ninth class and handed it over to Kamal.

It was the first time Kamal had got new books. He soared to the top of the world. Reaching home, when Kamal told Kanta and Madan about his new books, they both felt that a great burden had lifted off their chests.

'Kamal's teacher must indeed be some god,' Kanta said, overcome with gratitude.

'When god wants to give something to a man, He gives it through a fellow man. Our Kamba is lucky,' Madan endorsed Kanta's opinion.

That day Kamal realized that he had indeed achieved some success, because the third position in the eighth class exam had solved his problem of buying books for the ninth class. But his parents said it was god's mercy. That might well be true, he thought.

Studies for the ninth class had begun in earnest. Kamal went to his school regularly. Tarsem came home on leave after three-four days. The same day Kamal went to his house and told him all about his eighth class result and the new books that he had got for the ninth.

'Yes, I know Master Banarsi Dass. He is a noble soul. He has an only son and wanted to educate him but that was not to be. The boy became a loafer and has taken to smoking bidis and cigarettes. That boy! He is on all sorts of intoxicants! He is the opposite of his father. By giving you books, Masterji sees in you his own son. In helping you, he might derive the joy of educating his own son.'

'That cannot be true. Masterji loves me for what I am.' Kamal thought as he patiently listened to Tarsem.

Master Banarsi Dass grew fonder of Kamal by the day as he saw him working hard.

* * *

Another two years went by. Kamal had passed the ninth and joined the tenth class. The tenth class exam was drawing near. Master Banarsi Dass was greatly worried for Kamal's sake as he knew that sitting for the Board exam required hard work. He sent for Kamal one day and said to him, 'Kamal, son, the tenth class exam is conducted by the Board. It's tough and you will have to work really hard.'

He asked him how many hours he studied at home. For Kamal that was a difficult question. On returning home from the school he had to attend to one chore or the other. They did not have electricity to study by. The earthen lamp burnt on kerosene oil which was a problem. Not only did it give off soot, but it also cost a lot. How could the family let it burn for long hours at night? The truth was that whatever Kamal could study, he studied at school. At home he could, at the most, do his homework.

He had to give some reply to Masterji. So he said, 'Sir, I study for a couple of hours during the day.'

'How can that be? I know you devote at least five-six hours to studies. Now you would have to study at least two hours more,' advised Master Banarsi Dass.

'Yes, sir. I'll do that,' Kamal assented.

Lingering a while more with his teacher, he bid him namaste and left the place to return home.

'Did Master Banarsi Dass really believe what I told him? How will I study for that long at home? I was only agreeing to what he said,' Kamal was bothered on his way home.

He reached home at half past two. In the absence of his mother, he served himself a meal and sat down to eat. Kamlesh was busy studying. Usha and Louku too were doing their homework, their school bags placed before them on the mud floor.

'Where has Mother gone?' Kamal asked Kamlesh on finishing his meal.

'We saw her going with her sickle towards the ravine to cut saroot grass. Father has to go out for work every day, she said. He does not have time. She said she would herself bring home small quantities of saroot grass everyday so that we have enough of it to thatch the roof of the hut,' Kamlesh replied.

Kamal knew that their hut was in very bad shape and they would have to live in it during the rains. At least one layer of thatching grass was required to keep it from leaking. That had made his mother go by herself to the ravine.

Without a second thought, Kamal took hold of another sickle and set out to join his mother. It was a matter of minutes before he was cutting ripe grass stocks by his mother's side. Both son and mother made bundles they could carry.

The sun was setting now. Raising their bundles onto their heads, they started their homeward journey. It took them several days to gather sufficient saroot grass for thatching their hut. Kamal availed of this opportunity to collect tinder wood also for the family kitchen from the waste land where the village cattle went to graze. At times, he would bring back sackfuls of dried dung-cakes, which came in handy as fuel.

Two more years passed in this manner. Age had begun to leave its marks on both Madan's and Kanta's withered faces. Kanta's hair was turning grey. Madan's temples were touched with silver. Kamal had passed the tenth and eleventh class exams during this period and had taken the twelfth class exam as well. He had also gone to the city of Jammu to sit for a competitive exam for admission to an engineering college.

Kamal took time off his studies to help his parents in household chores and tutoring the promising students of his village to meet his pocket expenses. He had also set aside some money to buy books for himself.

The exams were over and farmers had started sowing for the autumn harvest. They supplemented the rainwater in their fields with their supply from the canal. Madan's family was busy planting on the one-fourth contract. Now both Kamal and Kamlesh could sow paddy like any other adult. The family kept enough paddy to meet its year's requirement of rice and sold the rest to buy a suit of coarse cotton for each member of the family.

The work in the field which Madan's family was planting was to finish in a day or two when Shammi, daughter of Kamal's *taya*⁴ suddenly came to them. Keening, she said, 'Dadaji has expired.'

On hearing about Sardari Lal's demise, both Kamal and Madan began to cry and reached the home of the deceased in tears.

Sardari Lal's last rites were performed on the river bank at noon the following day. For the next ten days they had a stream of visitors who came to pay their condolences. Kanta and Madan had to stay on for the whole duration which was a great hardship for Madan's family. He was in a quandary: all those days in mourning were compulsory, but who would feed his family during that time?

* * *

4. Father's elder brother.

About the Author and the Translator

Author

SHAILENDER SINGH was born in the Chhamb valley and had a liberal upbringing. A large part of his childhood was spent in refugee camps and tents in the process of migrations and upheavals. Unrest in the region interrupted his engineering degree education which later culminated in a postgraduate degree in Jammu. A trained Border Security Force commando, Shailender writes at night. He has two novels in Dogri *Hashiye Par* (2010) and *Sewadhani* (2012). His primary concerns are to creatively interpret the lives of the socially oppressed and underprivileged sections of society. Presently he is a Superintendent of Police in Jammu and Kashmir.

Translator

SUMAN K. SHARMA hails from Mirpur, a town of Jammu and Kashmir which is now under the control of Pakistan. He was brought up in Jammu where his family settled after the 1947 riots in the state. Dogri is his language from infancy. After schooling, he studied English literature at the University of Jammu. He has been writing since his student days, contributing articles to national dailies and magazines on topical issues, and spends his leisure translating Dogri poems and excerpts of Dogri literature into English. In 2000, he has published a novel, *Vagabond* (Writers' Workshop). It was around that time when he took up Dogri-English translation seriously and published *Tales from the Tawi* (Publication Division, Government of India, 2005). He also published a novel in Hindi, *Badalte Padaav*. His translation of Mohan Lal Sapolia's short story won the prize in a short story competition organized by the Sahitya Akademi during its Golden Jubilee Year in 2007.

The result of Kamal's twelfth class exam was declared. He had himself travelled to the town to look at the Board's gazette. To his surprise, he had outdone his classmates, passing the exam in the first division. No other student from his school had ever scored first class marks. He had proved to the whole town that the son of an unlettered labourer could pass the twelfth class exam in the first division.

Kamal's success became a matter of discussion among students and teachers alike. His family in the meantime was passing through hard days. Madan resumed work after the mourning period somehow or the other and Kamlesh looked after the home. Because of all the strain, she caught a cold. It took the family quite a few days to revert to normalcy.

From his classmates Kamal learnt that there were just five days to apply for admission in a college in Jammu. Kamal decided that he would seek admission on Saturday itself, before the last date.

It was Kamal's third trip to Jammu. He had been there earlier first to fill up the form for the entrance exam to engineering college and then to sit for this same exam.

He had left word at home that after his college admission, he would be staying with Tarsem at his in-laws' home. Tarsem's wife, who was his aunt, had affectionately insisted that he stay with them at her parents' home in Jammu.

Kamal arrived at the college, collected the form and filled it up. He learnt from some boys that the result of the entrance test for engineering college was to be declared by five the same evening and if there was any delay, it would be published in the morning papers the following day. Kamal was hopeful as he had done well in that exam.

'If I deposit the admission fee in this college and afterwards get selected for the engineering college, then that amount would go waste,' Kamal thought. 'I had better wait for another day to seek admission here as there is still some time left.' Having so decided, he reached the home of Tarsem's in-laws, which was more than a kilometre away.

Kamal told Tarsem how he had decided to wait for a day before he secured admission in the city college since the result of the admission test for engineering college was also expected that very evening. Tarsem agreed that it was the right decision, since he would not know even if the admission results of the engineering college were to be declared that evening, and would in any case have to wait for the morning newspapers carrying the result.

Suppressing his anxiety, Kamal had his dinner and went to sleep.

He got up early in the morning the following day when it was still dark and his hosts were asleep. The wait for the newspaper made him impatient and he decided to go out in search of one.

Kamal left his bed and without disturbing anyone, opened the door quietly to step out of the house. In fifteen minutes he was at the spot near the bus-stand where a number of men were busy carrying stacks of newspapers. It was from here that newspapers were dispatched every morning to various places in and around the city. Kamal bought a copy and fervently scanned every single page. In the middle of the paper was a page devoted to the results of the engineering college entrance exam.

It did not take Kamal long to see his name: third from the bottom. His spirits soared and for a moment he felt as if he was floating. Paper in hand he rushed back to the house where he was staying and going straight to Tarsem, he broke the news to him, 'Chachu,' he said breathlessly, 'the engineering college entrance exam result is out and I have been selected. Look here!'

Tarsem sat up in bed and eagerly took the paper from him. Excitedly, he called out his wife and said, 'Rani, our Kamal has cleared the entrance exam to the engineering college.'

Along with Rani, the others in the house also heard Tarsem. Beaming with happiness for his sake, they all congratulated Kamal. They also felicitated Rani and Tarsem for having encouraged Kamal.

Tarsem felt proud of Kamal. Now there would be a big officer in his clan. They could proudly say that they had an engineer in the family. He knew that getting Kamal into the engineering college in Srinagar would be an enormous expense which he would himself have to bear. He began to plan how he would arrange that kind of money.

Then he looked at his older daughter Komal, who studied in the fifth class. Tarsem dreamt that one day little Komal too would pass such an exam and enter a reputed college or university.

Kamal longed to reach home. Reach home and tell Mother. Tell Father. Tell his younger siblings of his success. He was impatient. But Rani insisted that he could leave only after breakfast.

Kamal had his breakfast and bidding namaste to everyone, almost ran to the bus-stand to take a bus back to his village. The rickety old bus halted at every stop to either pick up or drop passengers, which irritated him and added to his eagerness to reach home. But the bus moved at its own speed and reached the town after more than two hours. By that time the sun had reached its zenith.

As Kamal walked from the village bus-stop to his home, his eagerness to display the fireworks of his happiness to his family did not give him time to notice who was walking ahead of him or who trailed.

Only Usha and Louku were at home.

'*Vir*[5] has come!' Louku exclaimed on seeing Kamal. A strapping boy who had left his childhood far behind, Louku could not help giving a childish whoop on seeing his eldest brother returning home.

'Where is Mother?' Kamal asked him after looking for her here and there.

'Mother has taken Kamlesh *didi* to the doctor. Father is not home since morning. He too has gone to work,' Louku replied even before Usha could open her mouth.

'What's wrong with Kamlesh?' Kamal asked anxiously as she had seemed well when he left home, except for a cough and fever.

'Didi was coughing badly and was also running a high fever,' Louku again preempted Usha.

Kamal decided to go to the town to meet Mother and Kamlesh.

'Do you know I have passed the engineering college admission exam! The result was in today's paper,' Kamal exclaimed to Usha and Louku before leaving, and gave the paper to Usha to see for herself.

They both began to jump for joy. Louku went on shouting,' Vir has become an engineer!'

'I will go fetch Kamlesh and Mother,' Kamal said to his siblings and proceeded towards the town.

Usha was in the ninth class and could read English. She had also got the third rank in her classes. She spread the pages and looked for her brother's name.

---

5. Adulatory term for an older brother.

By that time the newspaper had also reached the town's bazaar and the educated among the shopkeepers had seen the results. There were many boys from the town who had sat for the entrance exam but only Kamal had been selected. The town's students had already read that the son of a fisherman who also worked as a daily wager, had won a seat in an engineering college.

Nearly everyone in the school teachers and students alike knew Kamal by face. But the people in bazaar had only just come to hear about him. They did not know him personally.

Kamal reached the government dispensary.

The doctor in charge gave them some tablets and told Kamlesh and Kanta to buy the rest from the market. As they left the dispensary, Kamal felt that Kamlesh's face had turned a sickly pale. Her eyes were sunken and there were dark patches under them. Lack of nourishment had left Kamlesh too thin for her height and her two-day illness had turned her into someone who looked as if she had been ailing for two months. Kamlesh was happy when she saw Kamal coming to the hospital from the direction of the bazaar. A little smile played on her lips.

'Mother, what has happened to Kamlesh? Such decline in just a day?' Kamal asked.

'Yesterday, around midnight, she began coughing violently and by the morning she had developed high fever,' said Mother.

'What does the doctor say, Mother?' Kamal asked.

'The doctor has given these medicines and told us to buy some others from the bazaar. Even if we don't buy them, she'll be all right with these,' Kanta said, showing him the medicines in her palm.

Kamal understood that Mother told him not to go to the bazaar for the medicines which came at a price.

'Mother, I have not touched the money saved on my college fees. We can buy medicines for Kamlesh,' he said.

At that Kanta handed over the prescription to him. Now they were in front of the chemist's shop. As they entered the shop, Kamlesh and Kanta sat on a bench while Kamal handed over the prescription to the chemist.

'Kamal is a good boy. His father, poor fellow, sells fish to make both ends meet. But the son has brought fame to the whole region,' a man was saying to the shop owner.

'So many boys from the town's school had taken the exam, but not one of them had made the score except he. Till now, only the son of Bihari of the sawmill ever cleared that exam. That too after studying in a Jammu school and supported by private tutors! But Kamal studied in this very school and qualified in the engineering entrance exam. He has brought honour not only to the school but to the whole town,' said the shop owner.

Seated on the bench, Kamlesh and Kanta were all ears. Kamlesh was elated on hearing that her brother would be going to an engineering college. For a few moments she forgot her own sickness and swam in a sea of happiness, her sickly face taking on a glow of pride.

Kanta too was very happy, though she couldn't trust her ears. Along with her daughter Kamlesh she watched Kamal paying for Kamlesh's medicines.

When he turned back, he saw his mother and sister looking at him with adoration. Kamal could read Mother's eyes; 'Kamal,' she was telling him wordlessly, 'you are indeed a true son."

Kamal forced a smile to his face and said nothing. Then the three of them started to walk to their home.

On the way Kamlesh coughed now and then.

Glancing at Mother's face, for the first time in his life Kamal felt proud of himself. He had achieved what none of his peers at the school could do; he had brought that sparkle of pure joy to her face.

On their way home, many villagers looked at them with awe.

* * *

His day's work over, Madan collected his wages and went to Desu Shah's shop to buy groceries.

'Come, Madan, how do you do? Congratulations! Your son has brought glory to all of us,' said the shopkeeper as he cast his eyes on Madan.

Madan did not quite know what to say.

'Countless boys sat for the exam to be admitted to the engineering college, but only your son was selected. He is our son too. Do please sit down,' Desu Shah said.

It was the first time ever that Madan had received so much respect at Desu Shah's shop. He sat down on the bench and it was only then that he could imagine the significance of what his son had attained. Exhausted after a day's hard labour, he was filled with a new energy and in a moment his weariness dropped away. Now he realized why most of the people in the bazaar were looking at him strangely.

'Madan, it takes money to become an engineer. But don't you worry. Everything will turn out well,' Desu Shah said forcing himself to smile.

On hearing about the expense, happiness drained from Madan's face, like a punctured tyre losing its shape. He began to worry how he would meet the cost of his son's study at a professional college in the city when he couldn't fund his studies in a small-town school. From where would he get all that money? Then there were his other children. He had to look after them too.

On the way back Madan was trying to find answers to these problems. He did not have any land or property worth the name which he could sell. If he failed to arrange the money, his son might lose his chance to become an engineer.

'No, no, that shouldn't happen! I shouldn't allow it' Madan said to himself and reached home.

Everyone was waiting for him at home. Today, they were not waiting for the rations he brought, but only to share with him their pride and their happiness. Kanta had been building castles in the air ever since noon.

'Bhapa, Bhapa, Vir has become an engineer,' Louka said to Madan as soon as he saw him.

'Vir has not become an engineer yet. He will have to study to be one,' said Usha correcting Louku.

On seeing Kamal home, a smile appeared on Madan's face, but then he became somber. Madan came to the tuala and sat with his family. Kanta had noticed and wondered why he was not as happy as everyone else around him. She stared at him unblinkingly for two-three minutes and realizing that Madan was deeply preoccupied, asked, 'What's wrong with you? Is everything okay?'

'Yes, it is,' replied Madan.

'Then why are you so silent? Are you unwell or feeling tired?' Kanta asked again.

The compulsions of prolonged malnutrition, scarcity of food, and overstretching his meagre bodily resources as a daily wager had aged Madan before his time.

'Well, now we have to arrange for Kamal's admission fee. It will take a lot to see him through engineering. We don't have anything which we could sell off to pay even for his admission,' said Madan, patting Kamal's back listlessly.

Madan's voice had dropped while he spoke and wrinkles of worry appeared on his forehead. He said, 'If we lose this opportunity for lack of funds....' He could not complete his sentence.

Kanta and Kamal also became pensive and the air in the house grew dense.

Kamal realized all over again that passing an exam did not by itself mean much. One got felicitations from people, some praise too, but nothing beyond that. Like his father, Kamal also began to sink into an ocean of worry, with no island of hope in sight.

The atmosphere of joy gradually turned into deep worry. Kanta also started thinking about the expenditure that Kamal's admission to an engineering college involved.

Madan had only one support—Tarsem. But Tarsem's means were limited. In the short span of his service, he had not been able to buy all that he himself needed, nor did he have a big bank balance.

But Tarsem had vowed to himself that he would help Kamal to pursue his studies. Well did he know that it was not merely helping out a needy relative but a wise investment. To spend on human development was the best form of investment ever and Kamal not only belonged to his community but also to the same family. Moreover, he had been coaching Kamal for the last ten-twelve years. In Kamal he saw a ray of hope for his entire family. Tarsem could not allow this opportunity to go waste. He had set apart a portion of his salary for the purpose.

Tarsem went through every detail to send Kamal to the engineering college at Srinagar. He got him two sets of shirts and trousers, a sweater, and a waistcoat. He gave him his own suitcase as well as a holdall. He went along with him to see him through his admission on time. When they left in the second week of August, everyone in the house came as far as the top of the road to say goodbye to them.

Kanta's eyes brimmed with tears since it was the first time Kamal was going so far away from her; he could not return before four-five months.

Madan lifted his baggage and loaded it onto the bus. When he came back home, they were still talking about Kamal. Kamal's younger siblings were sad at his departure.

Madan did not quite know how to express his gratitude to Tarsem. He simply said to his wife, 'Tarsem has done us many favours. It appears he has to pay us a debt of a previous life.'

'Many a time I feel that God has sent us Tarsem in the form of an angel,' said Kanta in agreement with her husband.

Tarsem and Kamal stayed that night at Jammu with Tarsem's in-laws and in the morning left for Srinagar in an eighteen-seater minibus on an eight-hour journey through mountainous terrain.

The Makings of a Tall Tree

The city of Srinagar is about three hundred kilometres from Jammu. With a population exceeding a million, it is the biggest city in the Kashmir Valley. Between the cities of Jammu and Srinagar lies the Peer Panchal range of mountains. The road travellers usually take between the two capital cities is the National Highway 1-A, that tunnels through the mountains and passes over the Chenab river and other streams. At Banihal, to the south of Kashmir, is the country's longest tunnel extending to two and a half kilometres. There also exists the historic Mughal route which the cattle-breeding communities of Gujjar-Bakkarwals take to cross the Peer Panchal range through minor passes during the summers and along which they return to Jammu with the onset of the winter season.

The pleasant climate of the Kashmir valley is entirely different from that of Jammu. In the winters, the valley sees snow and tourists from other parts of the country as well as many foreigners frequent the place. Every season brings its own charm here. The cup-shaped valley is called 'heaven on earth'.

The Dal is the biggest and the most beautiful lake of the Kashmir valley. To the east of the Dal Lake lie the Mughal gardens and the Chashma Shahi—the Royal Spring—monuments which still retain their beauty and utility. On the other side, on the west of Dal Lake, stands an important Muslim shrine, the Dargah Sharief. It houses a relic of Prophet Mohammed and is known as the Hazratbal Dargah.

On the southern side of the Dargah is situated an engineering college. The college runs a hostel for the out-of-town students.

Tarsem got Kamal admitted to the engineering college, found him accommodation in the hostel, and then returned to Jammu. It took Kamal some time to adjust to the new environment.

From the mosque attached to the shrine rose calls to the faithful to offer prayers five times a day. On his way to the college, Kamal frequently saw people leaving aside everything else to offer prayers at intervals all through the day.

If there was ever a slight increase in the temperature, it started to rain. The houses here had sloping roofs. The raindrops fell on the tin roofs with the music of *chhan chhan.*

Freshers were accommodated in the hostel two or three to a room. Kamal noticed that the room had wooden beds instead of cots. Each student was given a bed, a table, a chair, and an electric lamp fixed on the wall. The door of the room opened to the verandah and on the other side of the room was a big window which had glass panes as well as wire mesh on it. One could open or shut either of them as one liked.

Two or three rooms away, but inside the building itself, were located the toilets and the bathrooms. Hot and cold water was always available. Not far from the hostel lay the dining room with its long tables and rows of chairs so that everyone could sit together to dine.

Kamal had two companions in the room: One was Niraj from Jammu and the other, P. Raju from Andhra Pradesh. Niraj's friend, Jivan, lived in the opposite room along with two other boys. Jivan was also from Jammu. He had topped the list of the twelfth class candidates. Niraj too had scored over eighty per cent in the exam. Kamal's score was less than sixty-five per cent.

The college opened and the classes began. Jivan frequently came to Niraj and berated the hostel atmosphere, 'There is not enough time to study in this place. How can three boys live in a single room?'

'There is a problem with everything we do, friend. One has to go outside the room even for a bath or to relieve oneself,' Niraj said in agreement with Jivan.

'Niraj, my dear friend, we can put up with this somehow. But do you know the biggest problem that we are going to face? You won't find any private tutors here!' said Jivan.

Kamal sat listening to them. He thought to himself that life was comfortable enough in the hostel. Nicely-cooked meals were served on the table three times a day. Back home, six of his family lived in a broken down hut while here only three boys shared a well-appointed room. There, he had to share a cot with one or the other sibling of his but in this place he had a large bed to himself. Where once he had to study at night in the dim light of a kerosene lamp, and that too with the greatest economy, now, his room was awash with electric light all night. He recalled how all his books became wet and soggy during the rains, but here he lived in a brick and mortar room which had also been whitewashed with lime. A leak in the ceiling was unthinkable. There was no restriction on how long a student studied in his room after his classes. Most importantly, the college library was open till midnight with all the facilities made available.

Kamal began to study there till long after college hours, working hard with interest and devotion. All this time he did not have any contact with his family, except through an exchange of letters with Tarsem.

The first semester came to an end. The exam was fixed for the second week of the month of December. The month had already begun. It was biting cold in Srinagar. A room heater was installed in the room to keep it warm. At night, all the windows were closed and curtains drawn over them.

* * *

It was about seven in the morning. Kamal woke up to the noise in the hostel verandah. He poked his face out of the folds of the quilt. Niraj and Raju were not present in the room. Their beds were empty and the door stood open. There was great hullabaloo in the verandah as if a groom's party was setting out for the bride's place.

What's happening? I was studying late last night and didn't hear anything. There was nothing on the radio either.' Kamal wanted to know what the noise was about.

Flinging the quilt aside, Kamal lowered his legs to the floor, drew the slippers from under the bed with his foot and put them on. The slippers felt ice-cold to his feet. Then he got up. He drew aside the window curtain and looked out. The scene outside was awesome. Momentarily, he stood there motionless like a statue. Little wisps of snow dropped from the sky like swabs of cotton. The ground below was entirely covered with a white sheet. Fresh snow on the branches of a willow tree gave the top of a tree the comical shape of a man spinning cotton, with cotton stuck all over his head.

Snow falling on the tin roof did not make any sound and a calm prevailed in the environment. The entire scene looked unreal like a fantasy shot for a film on the paradise. For a few moments Kamal forgot himself. It was his first glimpse of snowfall. The scene gave him a joy he had never felt before.

Turning back, Kamal picked up his sweater from the chair and putting it on came outside the room and rushed happily to join his classmates who were dancing about and talking among themselves joyously.

Outside, all the pathways lay covered under a white sheet of snow. There was no grass to be seen, no plant, no raised point, no depression, no brick and no stone. It was just one level ground. Niraj and P. Raju, who had struck up a friendship with Kamal, were also there. They were also looking skywards to see the first snowfall of their lives.

'Let's go and have some tea in the canteen,' Niraj proposed to Kamal and P. Raju.

'Okay, let's go,' P. Raju agreed.

'Let's go,' Kamal also said happily.

The three room mates walked towards the canteen which was about two hundred metres from the hostel. They left their footmarks on the snow-covered earth as they proceeded. Snow was falling from the sky on their heads and shoulders. At brief intervals they shook themselves and jerked the snow on them to the ground. But a fraction of it stuck in their hair where it melted with the body-heat, giving them an exquisite cold sensation as the chilly water flowed down the neck to the torso. This novel experience added to the beauty of it all.

Enjoying the snowfall, they reached Haji's canteen in a few minutes.

Haji Sultan Mohammed was a sixty-five-year-old grey-haired man of medium stature. He wore a round prayer cap and a loose cloak-like *phiran* of woollen cloth to protect himself from the chill. A *kangri*[1] supplied all the warmth he required. After having cleaned the tin-roofed kiosk, he had set the water to boil in a huge kettle and was busy doing small chores before the customers arrived.

'Haji sahib, *assaalamu alaykum*—peace to you!' Kamal, Niraj, and P. Raju exclaimed almost in one voice.

'*Wa alaykum-us-salaam*—and peace to you!' Haji Sahib responded with a smile.

'Will we get a cup of tea in this cold?' Niraj asked.

'You will get it in a moment, sahib,' said the Haji.[2] Smiling, he lifted the kettle and in its place put a pan on the stove for making tea.

Haji Sultan's kiosk was somewhat warmer than outside because of the heat from his gas stove.

Seated inside the kiosk, Kamal and his friends could see the roofs of the college buildings which were covered under a ten-centimetre thick layer of snow.

'Here, sahib.' The Haji brought scalding tea in cups and saucers and served them. Steam wafted from the hot cups and rose to the roof. In the same manner, steam from the kettle also rose to touch the tin roof above. The roof had

1. A small wicker-covered clay pot to carry embers of coal. In winter, Kashmiris carry it about to keep themselves warm.
2. A Muslim who has successfully completed the Haj pilgrimage.

become warmer and the snow over it melted in the shape of drops.

Kamal brought the cup to his lips to take a sip of the hot tea. A drop of molten snow fell from the tin roof onto Kamal's right hand. It spread to a narrow circle on his skin and disappeared. A tiny portion of water also went to his eyes and face.

These little drops of water chilled not only his body but dampened his spirits as well. His happiness was gone in a moment. His laughing face became somber. The water drop took him back to the last monsoon at his home three hundred kilometres away. His home, where six persons lived in an old and worn out hut. After a rainfall of just two days, the thatch could not withstand the downpour. The roof had started leaking like a sieve. There was not a dry place even for a cot. Everything was wet. Even the firewood was damp and Mother had not been able to cook till late in the night. They had all sat on the wet floor waiting for the rain to stop. The little ones had fallen asleep sitting up. Pots and pans were kept in several places inside the hut to catch the dripping water. Even books were soaked though wrapped in a bundle and transferred from one place to another several times. Wetness had botched his notebooks, with the ink spreading all over the pages. Occasionally, when the rainfall intensified, it poured from the roof like water pouring from the pitcher over a *Shivalinga*.[3] The mud floor of the hut was thoroughly wet and marked by footprints on it when anyone walked about.

The pinched visage of his younger siblings and the helplessness that he had seen that day on the faces of his mother

3. Sacred stone which represents the divine energy of the Hindu deity, Lord Shiva. Traditionally, a water-filled pitcher with a small hole is installed over a Shivalinga to keep it moist.

and father visited him all over again. To this day the memory had the power to make Kamal feel helpless.

He wanted his starving family to have, instead of a worn-out hut, a brick-and-mortar house, comprising rooms like the rooms that he had in his hostel, with cement plastered walls and a cemented floor. Theirs should be a house with real windows that could be thrown open during summers and shut in the winters, unlike the *dreh*[4] in their hut which allowed wind to pass through freely all twelve months a year.

He wanted his house to have a gas stove instead of wood-burning chulha, which his mother should be able to put off after her cooking. Then the pots would not be blackened and she wouldn't have to squander time and energy scrubbing them. Kamal thought to himself, 'We buy rations for one day at a time. We don't have enough money to buy rations for a whole week. If someone falls sick in the family, we depend on free medicines from the hospital. We cannot afford to buy all the medicines the doctor prescribes.'

Kamal was in deep thought. Pained he was by such memories, but not deterred. Every time he came out of such moods with a stronger resolve to study more, to work even harder.

They finished their tea and got up to leave. Niraj made the payment to Haji Sultan and they walked back to their hostel, making and unmaking their footprints on the carpet of snow.

Niraj and Raju were happily talking to each other. Kamal was walking with them anxious and restless.

In the snowfall which continued unabated, Kamal was seeing the difficulties his family might be facing because of the

---

4. A wall-like structure made of cane, placed on—or hinged to—the opening of a hut.

rainfall in his own village. He was praying that the snowfall in Srinagar and rainfall in the plains should stop sooner rather than later. With these thoughts he reached his hostel room along with his friends.

He had been living in a pukka building for the last four months. From a rundown hutment he had reached a much better place. But after spending so many days in the hostel he knew in his heart that his home was still the same old and worn-out hut. This left him confused. The heavy snowfall reminded him painfully of his home and of all the problems that his family had to face on rainy days.

Entering the room, Raju switched on the room heater, jauntily removed his shoes and lay on the bed wrapping the quilt round himself. Kamal dragged a chair from under the table and sat on it.

'It is time for the news. Kamal, would you please switch on the radio,' Raju said from within the folds of his quilt.

Kamal turned to glance at Raju's watch lying on the table and picking up the radio, turned it on. The newsreader announced at the end of the bulletin, '… And now the weather. The Kashmir Valley is facing heavy snowfall, which is likely to continue for the next twenty-four hours. There are sundry clouds over Jammu and it will be dry during the next twenty-four hours. Namaskar.'

On hearing the weather forecast about Jammu, Kamal heaved a sigh of relief. He felt as if someone had saved his books from getting wet. He felt a sudden lightness of heart.

After that storm of worrisome thoughts had passed, Kamal's resolve to study harder became firmer. He could clearly see his path ahead now. It was to score higher marks in the exams and get himself a good job, then to run his family with his earnings and build a pukka house of brick, mortar, and of wood, with a reinforced concrete roof. His thoughts went beyond his family. What would happen to the other people of the village who were also poor? What would they do, they, who like his own family, stood waist high in the mire of poverty. Would they remain *hashiye par*—on the margins? But for how long?

The newscast had given him some reassurance. He stood up and got ready.

Nearly all the college boys were dancing in their rooms or outside the premises celebrating the first snowfall. A few students had brought out their cameras and were merrily clicking pictures of their friends. A few others were throwing snowballs at each other. Kamal had his breakfast and proceeded alone towards the library once again with his books.

Kamal's exams were over in the month of December. The college closed for the winter vacations. All the hostel boys began to go home. Having lived in the comfortable environment of his college for four-five months, Kamal also went to his village to stay with his family in their hut. It was the first time that he felt the difference between the life in a pukka house and his family's bare survival in a thatched hut.

Everyone who met Kamal showed him much more consideration and respect than they ever had before. Two months of vacation passed in this manner and the third began. In the evening many village children came to Kamal. They sat on the pieces of sacking they had brought with them and studied under his guidance. Some parents had given Kamal some money for teaching their wards. But he did not accept anything from those children whose parents earned their livelihood by hard manual labour.

Madan began to worry again about having to pay for Kamal's second semester. It was the second week of March.

One day, the village postman brought a sealed khaki-coloured envelope addressed to Kamal. Kamal received the mail and invited the postman to sit with him for a while. The postman too wanted to rest his legs but there was no place for him to sit down.

'Kamal Sahib, I have some more letters to deliver yet. I'll come some other day,' the postman said and went away.

Kamal tore off envelope at a corner and took out a couple of sheets from it. He read the first page and his face became radiant with happiness. The letter informed him of the date of admission for the fourth semester, as also the result of the previous semester. It also told him that he had scored the highest marks in that exam. Kamal was beyond himself with happiness.

Kamal then turned over to the second sheet appended to the letter. He glanced over it and jumped for joy. That was the claim-form for a scholarship for standing first in class. Filling up this form meant that he would be receiving enough money for his education. Now he wouldn't have to go to anyone to fund his studies.

Little Louku, Usha, and Kamlesh had never seen their elder brother happier.

'Vir, what's in the letter?' Louku drew near him and asked. Usha and Kamlesh also stood waiting for his response.

'I have stood first in the first semester. Not just that, I will also receive a scholarship to complete my studies. No need now for us to borrow money from anyone else,' Kamal said with a smile.

Sitting in the tuala, Kanta listened to her children. She was beside herself with joy. Her son had stood first. Her real surprise was that he would be receiving a scholarship. Kanta could not believe her ears.

'Our Kamba is lucky. God is very kind to him. He has listened to the prayers of us poor folk too!' Kanta uttered involuntarily.

Looking at Kamal, Kamlesh was also filled with zeal and confidence. 'I too will study hard like Vir and stand first in my class. I too must become an engineer.'

It was evening now. Madan had come home after a day's hard labour. Hearing the good news first from Kanta and then from Kamal, he felt very happy. 'Our Kamal is blessed with good fortune', he exclaimed.

That day Tarsem also came home late in the evening. When Kamal learnt of his arrival, he set out to meet him and share his happiness with his uncle. Madan and Kamlesh also followed him.

Kamal pulled out the envelope from his pocket and showed him the two-page letter. Tarsem's face beamed with satisfaction. He said, 'Kamal, many many congratulations to you. I was confident that you would stand first.'

'How, brother, how could you foresee his luck,' Madan said to Tarsem playfully. Shailo Ram, who was sitting close by, also broke into laughter.

'No, Brother Madan, I don't know what lies in his fate,' said Tarsem with deep thought. 'But I certainly know that if we plant a *peepal*[5] sapling in a flower pot where it gets neither enough water nor soil, it may still go on living, but will never reach its full potential. That tiny little potted plant would always be striving to root its way out of the constricting pot. But if by chance, it finds a tiny hole in the pot itself, through which it may connect with the earth through its smallest root to regularly draw its sustenance, I assure you my dear Madan,

5. Sacred fig—*Ficus religiosa*.

then nothing can stop the little plant from growing into a big tree.'

Madan could understand nothing from Tarsem's outpouring except that out of the morass in which his family had been stuck, a *kamal*[6] had bloomed. Though Kamlesh had fully grasped Tarsem's meaning, she could not understand how it was connected with her brother, Kamal.

Perhaps Kamal had understood that, after all, the potgrown peepal had managed to connect with the earth. That was all that was required for a tree to grow.

* * *

And thus began a new story ...

6. The lotus flower.